BIRD
WITHOUT A CAGE

BRANDON ZENNER

Chapter One
Thursday, 13 June, 1940

My shift began at five in the morning, and now, an hour later, the headlights of an arriving truck dispel the shadows through the open window. The barnyard odors of hay and feed, tobacco smoke from the soldiers, and the thousands of pine crates loaded with wartime supplies are all overtaken by the sharp fumes of petrol. The odd scents have permeated the walls and have even found their way to my metal desk in the back office, where my typewriter sits beside a stack of forms. At least back here, there's a window to let in a fresh breeze. Plus, it's far enough away from the clamor of arriving soldiers filling their inventories that my record player can be heard, making filing reports more enjoyable.

Mazas sits across from me, leaning back in his chair. "It's early, isn't it?" He lets out a waft of cigarette smoke, which drifts lazily before finding the open window. The rolled tobacco looks slender between his thick fingers.

"A bit," I say and go back to sorting papers. Half an hour passes, and more headlights appear. First, one truck, and then three cars traveling together. We wait and smoke. My dark hair keeps falling in front of my eyes whenever I look down at the typewriter keys, and I'm starting to think that Mazas is right to keep his hair trimmed close to his scalp. I flip the record to side B of Chopin's Nocturnes when I see Brissanet leading a sergeant toward the office through the plate glass door.

"Morning," the officer says. Brissanet hands me a tally of supplies the soldiers are loading on the back of their transports before turning to leave. For food; canned fish, crackers, bread, and cheese. Loads of cigarettes, bedding, a dozen pairs of socks, and three new helmets. And, of course, fuel. Our warehouse carries everything an army needs to function except for arms and ammunition. There isn't a single bullet to be found among us, the ninety men of our unit and the forty-five who were broken off from other units to come work in the warehouse. All available weapons are issued to the soldiers on the front lines, and none sparred for us in the warehouses. A grievous oversight, if you ask me, to not arm every capable hand.

The sergeant's eyes are spiderwebbed red, and he finds a pack of cigarettes in his front pocket and pats his side pockets for a match. Mazas offers his lighter.

"Got the order now." The sergeant pauses to puff the cigarette to life. "It came straight from Nancy."

I look up from my typewriter and catch Mazas looking back at me.

The sergeant continues, "As soon as I drew up our supply list, we came right here."

"Where are you ordered to go?" Mazas asks, a new cigarette dangling from his lips.

The man shrugs. "To leave Sarrebourg, with supplies to last for three days. Nothing further."

The door opens, and Brissanet leads another officer into the back room. "Two more have arrived," he says. "Looks like we'll have a busy morning." Brissanet is a few years older than myself and likes to brag that he can work double shifts without a problem. But the bags under his eyes show his exhaustion, and the scruff on his chin tells me he's not taking care of himself as he should. As I am third in command, I'll talk to Longchamps about giving Brissanet more than just a few hours to rest.

The ledger is passed to Mazas, and we wish the first sergeant safe travels as he grinds his cigarette out in the ashtray. He offers a halfhearted salute and turns to leave. The following official tells us he was given the same orders to pull back with enough supplies to last his men three days.

"It's the horses that concern me," the man says, brushing a palm over his unkempt mustache. "If we get held up somewhere, I'll have no choice but to let them go. Or put them down. Better to be neutralized than be offered to the Wehrmacht."

We ask him the usual questions about the fighting in the north. Have the

Germans made new ground? Did last month's offensive go as poorly as rumors suggest? Is Paris really declared an open city to reduce destruction in the event the Germans make it that far south? He raises his hands in a futile gesture. It isn't possible that the Germans have broken through Belgium, up to the Ardennes, and are now in our country.

The officer shakes his head and says something that is not shocking—yet officers rarely discuss such personal opinions with lesser ranks. "If only the damn Third Republic extended the Maginot Line. The Germans would be pushed back to Berlin, no problem." We type as he continues, "It will go down as the biggest blunder in French history, perhaps in the history of the world. Why didn't the politicians consider the Germans to invade in the same manner as the last war when even children aren't so blind? By God, the Ninth and Second divisions weren't even dug-in when the Panzers rolled over their defenses. And the counterattack … the largest tank battle in history, and still, it did little to halt Germany's progress."

We don't answer. The dilemma of how unprepared we were for the attack and how we learned nothing after the first war is a common and frustrating topic. However, the Nazi war machine is also fighting the Russians in the east and spread thin. Hope remains.

The officer takes his leave, and as the morning hours pass, soldiers continue to arrive by bus, car, truck, and horse. They've all been given similar orders from command in Nancy to leave right away. My fingers ache. I can't type as fast as Mazas, and he sometimes jokes about me pecking at the keys, but I haven't stopped since dawn. I wonder how he can type so fast. His fingers are like sausages smacking at the keyboard, yet his broad palms conduct symphonies over the keyboard. I stop to check my watch and see that it's noon. "Hungry?" I ask, snapping Mazas from his feverish typing.

"Hmm?" he says. "As a matter of fact, I am." His eyes are red and weary, and he rubs the stubble on his chin.

I open two cans of sardines and find my canteen. I pass an open tin, careful not to spill oil on the papers and ledgers. The door opens, and a rush of noise invades our solitude, along with a waft of petrol fumes. Brissanet enters and drops off three inventory lists. "I've never seen it so busy. Have you?"

We both shake our heads, and I peer outside the window. The lot is full. I place the tin down and start typing. Hours pass, and the paperwork never ceases. It's near evening when a soldier arrives who has traveled all the way from Nancy, nearly ninety kilometers to the west. He, too, was given orders to evacuate. I ask him, "Why drive east to Sarrebourg if you are to journey south?" I assume he, like most others, will be traveling to Epinal, Dijon, or Besançon.

The officer holds a cigar clamped in his teeth, protruding past a thick beard. "We're boarding a train in Saverne. I got sixty men on foot, with no trucks."

At six o'clock, Voulard and Billet arrive to relieve our shifts. They both hold cups of coffee, and Voulard is eating a pastry. Working in the warehouse, surrounded by enough food to feed thousands, has made Voulard's sides wider and his cheeks rosier. Joining the army did little to reduce his obesity. I often wonder how he would hold up in a tactical unit. Most of our company is just as fit as a fighting brigade, myself even more so than many soldiers I encounter. My years of gymnastics, performing handstands and balancing acts on the streets of Paris have carved my body into solid, lean muscle. Mazas is a little shorter than myself, yet his shoulders are wide and his biceps thick.

I rub at the aches in my palms and wrists, and Mazas and I leave to find Brissanet. We pass Lieutenant Serre on the way out. The wrinkles engraved on the old man's face look to have deepened, and he doesn't have his customary pipe clamped between his teeth. "Mazas," he says, his upper lip involuntarily wiggling his gray mustache. "Zenner. Be back at twenty-one hundred."

"Yes, sir," Mazas and I say in unison, and the lieutenant brushes past us without offering further detail.

"Have you ever seen the warehouse so busy?" Mazas asks as we weave through throngs of worried-looking soldiers. Young and old, and from various branches and backgrounds. Teachers, farmers, sons, and husbands, all having left their lives behind to repel the barbarian invaders from our soil once again. Many fought in the last war, and the fatigue is forever engraved in their tired expressions. Years spent in muddy trenches, surrounded by engrossed rats, lice, decomposing corpses, and the never-ceasing rainfall of bullet fire, artillery, and actual downpours of rain, drove them to the brink of madness. Now, they're fighting again. I was too young to fight in the last war, but my stepfather was not. He never spoke of the battles. Never said a word. I've since learned of the terrible conditions from passing servicemen who had also served, survived, and now fight again.

I reply to Mazas, "The last time it was close to this busy was during the May offensive." Our warehouse in Sarrebourg is far enough away from the fighting in the north that the chance of seeing actual warfare is slim. In many ways, our unit—the twenty-third Company of Intendance—is lucky to have been assigned desk jobs. Yet, we're helpless as rumors of Germany's victories spread down the line, and the occasional advantageous counterattack is given by enthralled servicemen. Yes, our lives are spared from fighting, yet we yearn to be a part of France's liberation, to protect our families and homes. However, we were given typewriters instead of rifles only because we scored high on vocabulary tests when joining the military.

We find Brissanet waiting by the exit, leaning against the wall and yawning. When he opens the door for us to leave, I say, "My God." Dozens of vehicles are parked in front of the warehouse, and traffic jams the road. But that isn't what startles me; it is the highway far in the distance, packed with vehicles heading south. Never has the road seen such clutter.

"Let's get to town," Brissanet urges.

Mazas and I agree. We distance ourselves from the warehouse and cross the cow pastures. The farmers had given us trouble long ago when we trampled through their fields, using them as a shortcut, and Lieutenant Serre instructed us to use the road. But as time passed, and we promised not to damage the barbed-wire fencing or let any cows loose, which has happened more than once, the locals relented. Now, when we meet the farmers by chance in the fields, we offer them chocolate bars or the occasional bottle of champagne taken from storage. There are perks to working in the warehouse.

"You think the Germans will break the line?" Brissanet asks as we see the glow from the town's streetlights ahead.

"They already have," Mazas answers. "Dunkirk and Calais have fallen. If Paris has been declared an open city, the Germans have indeed made progress further south."

"No," Brissanet says. "I mean the Maginot Line, east of us."

"No," I say. Brissanet has a reputation for asking obvious questions. We are all afraid that the Germans will attack head-on, in which case, we are near the border. But as expected, they invaded through Belgium. "If they were going to attack Strasbourg, they would have by now."

The path turns to pavement, leading to homes, shops, and businesses.

Store owners stand outside, wiping their palms on their aprons and talking to soldiers. People amble by, carrying boxes, crates, bottles of wine, wheels of cheese, and loaves of bread. Men wear caps low over their eyes, striding purposefully along the sidewalks. Once we cross the Saar River bridge, we reach the open square lined with restaurants and shops. A few days a week, the road is closed, and local businesses set up booths running the broad side of the cathedral. I visited the church once to see the architecture; the smooth carved wood, chiseled stone columns, and intricate stained-glass windows. I didn't stay for mass like many soldiers regularly do, but the workmanship is admirable. Nothing like the cathedrals in Paris, but still lovely.

"Zenner," I hear from behind me and turn to see Batist. He waves for us to halt and says something to a soldier beside him. Then he walks quickly toward us, taking a long pull from a beer bottle. "Did you hear? The police, they're gone."

"The police?" Mazas says. "What do you mean, gone?"

"They've vacated the office and burned all their files before leaving. The officials are doing the same. Look." He points up the street over the busy flood of apprehensive-looking soldiers purchasing supplies, beer, and coffee. "The smoke from the chimneys. They're burning papers."

"How do you know?" I ask.

"I saw it. Go take a look yourself."

He's telling the truth, but I don't want to believe officials are fleeing the city.

"Let's get something to eat," Mazas says, looking away from the smoke.

We go to our usual café, but they are out of tripe, so I order steak cooked in butter, the only meat they have left. The steam wafting off the meat is laced with sage, and the butter sauce is savory with the cooked juices. We finish our meals, drain back beers, and Brissanet says, "I think we should head back." We all agree. The urgency of the townspeople, the worried conversations, and the curious glances at the flow of traveling soldiers make me uneasy. Plus, we should report the news of the police leaving the city to Lieutenant Serre, although he likely knows.

We hurry back to the warehouse in complete darkness, careful of the soft pasture and mounds of cow dung. The traffic to the warehouse has doubled, and the parked vehicles spill onto the grassy fields around the paved flattop.

Motorcycles, bicycles, and horses tethered to bumpers are among the assemblage. My head feels light, breathing in the thick exhaust fumes.

We walk down the ample avenues in the warehouse, past thousands of crates, hay bales, helmets, and clothing boxes. A stopper opens the rear door, and light casts out to the catwalk.

Voulard and Billet are busy at their typewriters, but they scoot their chairs over when we arrive, and we squeeze together. Lieutenant Serre sits before a table full of ledgers and speaks on a telephone. Voulard shoots me a grave look and motions with his eyes to the lieutenant. Apparently, we missed a meaningful conversation with whomever he is speaking to. Just as I take a seat, he sets the receiver down and sighs out loud while rubbing the bridge of his nose. After finding his pipe on the table and packing tobacco in the bowl with his thumb, he says, "That was Nancy. They expect the arriving soldiers will lessen overnight. We've been given orders to vacate in the morning."

The typing stops altogether, and all eyes fall on the commanding officer as he strikes a match and puffs the tobacco to flame. "If Paris falls, the Wehrmacht will make their way south and east in record time."

He exhales a cloud and looks very old. Like the thousands of other elderly men who fought in the last war, Lieutenant Serre has returned to the armed forces to achieve victory for France once again, leaving his farm in the care of his wife and daughters. He clamps his pipe between his teeth and looks like he's about to offer consoling words to the worried men. But instead, he says nothing.

Chapter Two
Friday, 14 June, 1940

Voulard is smoking a cigarette beside the open window. "The traffic hasn't stopped," he says, turning to me. I stand and stretch my back, then roll up my blanket. We both slept in an empty office, going to bed near three in the morning. Now it's seven.

"You sleep at all?" I ask.

"Who can sleep with such noise?"

Sheer mental exhaustion helped me slip into a light and fragmented sleep, but the constant roar from the far-off road and the trucks rumbling to the warehouse never ceased.

Voulard grinds his cigarette on the windowsill and tosses the twisted end in an ashtray. "Let's get some coffee," he says.

I nod in agreement, and we step outside the office.

The warehouse is scrambling with activity, yet less crowded than the previous night. My head grows dizzy watching the frenzy of soldiers gathering supplies, everyone speaking at once so that the enormous room vibrates. Luckily, the bathroom is vacant, and I'm afforded a few moments of solitude. Cold water over my face revives me, but the steaming cup of coffee that Voulard hands me outside is more invigorating.

He enters the bathroom as I walk to the office alone, sipping the coffee. The tin cup is scorching, and I'm careful not to burn my lips.

As I enter the room, I notice that the typewriter clatter has ceased and the usual melodic classical music is not playing from my record player—which I keep in the office for all to use. A radio issues a static-filled broadcast from the rear desk, and all necks crane in that direction as if the broadcast holds a physical presence.

"What's going on?" I ask the room.

Longchamps hushes me down with a palm wave and whispers, "Zenner, come here." I walk to him and accept a cigarette from his open pack. Lieutenant Serre is sitting beside the radio, his pipe clamped between his teeth, his eyes a more vivid red than the burning cinder of his tobacco.

The lieutenant looks at me through the fog of smoke. "Italy's declared war." It comes as no surprise, yet the sting is sickening.

"Those bastards," I say, and listen to the announcer tell of Germany's victory in Poland, the Netherlands, Belgium, and half of France. The room is quiet, other than the occasional quip of disgust.

As the broadcast continues, I'm relieved to notice the stack of files has lessened. The door opens, and we all turn to see Ross walk in carrying a woven basket. His expression displays trepidation. "Sarrebourg is a mess," he says. "I had to walk to the far side of town to find an open bakery. Everything is shut down. Blinds are drawn on the homes, and some have nailed boards across windows and doors." He places the basket on a desk and doles out fresh bread. Though we have access to more food and supplies than a single person could eat in a lifetime, packaged goods and week-old bread are inedible compared to what the nearby boulangeries bake.

I tear off a chunk and bite into the chewy crust.

"All right," Lieutenant Serre says and lowers the radio volume. "Everyone, get back to work."

Heads turn to desks, and the lieutenant stands and leaves us to our tasks. I relieve Weber, whose eyes are swollen with exhaustion. He stands with a stretch and yawn and scratches his mess of hair. Although the line of vehicles visible from outside the window has thinned, the roar from the highway is louder than ever.

I go about my work, getting lost in the words, numbers, tallies, and names. All meaningless stuff, meant to be delivered to Nancy's personnel, whose job is to resupply our warehouse. Not an hour passes before Sergeant Longchamps flings the door open, says, "Zenner. Mazas," and motions for us to follow. We both stand and walk behind the towering man, fast down the hall. Longchamps would have made a great infantryman if not assigned to the warehouse. Out of all of our unit, he most resembles a soldier. That is to say, he's tall and strong, with short blond hair and an old scar running down his cheek. He's told us that the injury occurred from falling off a horse when he was a child, yet in the army, all scars and injuries become marks of honor and sacrifice. The Germans go so far as to have their cadets duel each other with sharpened fencing swords so they can proudly display facial scars later in life.

"What's going on?" Mazas asks.

Longchamps nods us forward. "This way."

We enter Lieutenant Serre's office. The old man sits behind his desk, rubbing the bridge of his nose. "I got the call," he says. Longchamps and I sit while Mazas stands in the rear. "Our outfit is to leave at once."

A sensation akin to a hot chill covers my skin, and I say, "Where are we ordered to go?"

After a pause, Longchamps responds for the lieutenant, "We're ordered to evacuate south. No further orders were given on where or how to get there."

It takes a moment to process that the French army is in complete disarray. It takes even longer to fully realize how dire our situation is and how prepared the German army is to mobilize all of France.

"There are responsibilities to tend to," Lieutenant Serre says from inside his smoke cloud, addressing Longchamps, who is second in command. "Nancy has instructed us to bring the tally sheets, so have them packed. Order the men to burn everything else."

"Yes, sir," Longchamps replies.

"The only way I see us all getting out together is by train, but I've spoken to the rail master in Sarrebourg, and their locomotives have either left or are at maximum capacity. I've been making calls to Saverne, but the telephone in their station just keeps ringing. Zenner, I may need you to travel there. Stand by. For now, you and Mazas help Longchamps. Have the men gather supplies for three days, and Zenner, pack a typewriter." He glances at us with heavy eyes and says, "Dismissed."

We turn and leave. Out in the hallway, I again ask, "Where are we going?"

"I don't know," Longchamps says. "South. Away from Paris."

"It doesn't feel right." Mazas shakes his head. "Leaving. Everything we've done here, all the records we've typed, day after day … we're to destroy them all and flee." He makes a clicking sound with his mouth. "Why abandon the warehouse for the Germans to plunder? Better they send munitions and let us dig fortifications."

Mazas would excel in the fighting ranks. We all would, except for Voulard, of course, and Piffet. Voulard is too large, and Piffet is too thin—like a skeleton. But the rest of us could give the Germans a bit of sport.

Longchamps shakes his head. "The army isn't sending munitions, so you can get that out of your head. I was in the office when Nancy called. From what I understand, they couldn't get supplies to us if they tried. The roads are inundated with evacuees, and railways and bridges are being destroyed to halt the German advance."

We're silent, contemplating that our lifeline to Nancy is severed.

Back in the office, Longchamps hastens the men into working order. The sheets and documents, which have cramped our fingers and caused our heads to swell, hour after hour, week after week, are being gathered and dumped into an empty steel drum brought in from the warehouse and placed beside the open window. Brissanet strikes a match, sets a rolled-up paper to flame, and then leans in the drum to start the fire. Dark, greasy smoke emerges and fogs the room. Months' worth of typed words are erased like a thumb over wet ink.

I bring five men at a time to the warehouse to gather supplies for three days. Everyone takes extra clean socks, and some change out of their old uniforms for new ones, leaving piles of scattered clothing. We pack tins of sardines, crackers, bottles of champagne, and dozens of cartons of cigarettes. We can trade the tobacco on the road if necessary, so we take more than any one of us could smoke in a lifetime.

It's nearing ten in the morning when Lieutenant Serre emerges from his office, pipe smoke trailing behind, and calls for Longchamps, Mazas, and myself. We gather in the hall as the men continue packing, burning papers, and whispering to each other in worried tones. "Where are we going?" they say, and, "How close are the Germans?" The radio gives little indication.

"I got ahold of the rail master in Saverne," Lieutenant Serre tells us. "All their cars have left, and besides, it's twenty kilometers away. Longchamps, come with me. We need to requisition trucks. You two, make sure the men are ready to vacate at a moment's notice. We depart as soon as we have automobiles."

With that, the lieutenant and Longchamps leave.

I swallow back a lump in my throat and feel the pressing need to be far from Sarrebourg. If the Wehrmacht is as close as presumed, they will soon come storming through our town to connect with reserves on the boundary and take the strategic city of Strasbourg.

Mazas and I go to our tasks, burning papers, gathering supplies, and preparing our backpacks. The men are soon ready, and the thick smoke in the office makes everyone's eyes tear. It isn't long until we hear an engine rumble into the lot. Mazas and I hurry outside to find the lieutenant stepping out from the passenger side door of a large civilian Renault truck.

"Zenner," he says. "How many of the men can drive a lorry?"

I think it over, but Longchamps shouts from the driver's seat, "Five that I know of. Six, including me."

"I can," Mazas adds.

"All right," the lieutenant says and turns to Longchamps. "Get three other drivers." He then addresses Mazas and me. "We found four abandoned trucks in Sarrebourg. That's enough to carry … close to a hundred when packed. Maybe a few more. You two will go with the first convoy. Pick twenty-five men to stay behind with me. I'll find them a way out."

"Sir," Mazas says, "I volunteer to stay behind and help organize the men."

"Me too, sir," I add.

"No," the lieutenant says. "I'm ordering the bulk of the company to move out. Longchamps will be the head officer, and I need you two to be his eyes and ears. He'll need your help, and I need to know reliable men are leading the others. Head first to Saverne, where regiments that have fallen back from the fighting in the north are regrouping. You'll be rerouted, I'm sure, somewhere south, but at least you'll be safe until further orders are given. If Saverne is unreachable, you must make decisions as you go. I will not tolerate more talk of staying behind."

"Yes, sir," we say in unison.

Longchamps emerges from the warehouse with three drivers. They quickly depart to Sarrebourg as the lieutenant heads to his office.

"Let's ready the men," Mazas says to me, watching the truck kick up a cloud of dust as it accelerates away.

"How should we pick the twenty-five who are to stay behind?"

"We can ask for volunteers."

"All will volunteer," I say.

"Then we'll make a lottery. Come."

I nod. "At least we have a destination."

"Indeed," Mazas agrees. "Saverne is twenty kilometers away."

"Closer to thirty."

"We'll be there in no time."

"Yes," I reply. "No time at all."

Chapter Three
Dijon

We hear engines outside and watch through the window as three trucks turn off the road and advance toward the warehouse. The Renault from earlier is in the lead, with two others in tow.

"They're back," I tell Mazas, who's stacking the last of the ledgers into wooden crates.

"That's it then." He stands and faces me. "Let's go."

I fling my half-smoked cigarette to join the smoldering embers in the metal drum, and we leave. The rest of the unit waits outside, shouldering large backpacks and standing beside or sitting on crates of supplies and files. Three soldiers left for town while the trucks were being rounded up and managed to commandeer a motorcycle to serve as a liaison, along with a small Citroen, which will lead the procession.

Lieutenant Serre emerges from the warehouse and hustles to the gathering. "Where's the fourth truck?" he asks Longchamps.

"It's gone."

"What do you mean?"

"Someone must have taken it."

I spy the lieutenant from the corner of my eyes; his pale face grows wearier, if that is at all possible. He takes the extinguished pipe from his teeth and taps the ash to scatter in the wind. More men must stay behind and find an alternative method to flee Sarrebourg.

Lieutenant Serre turns to the unit. "We're going to draw straws. Quickly, now."

A hand raises from the group. "I'll stay," the soldier says.

"Me too." Another hand raises, and then another. The gesture repeats itself, and soon Mazas tells the men that there are enough volunteers and the rest must board the trucks. An orderly panic ensues as the soldiers hoist crates and find cramped seats on the flatbeds. Those who are staying behind help the others.

Lieutenant Serre calls Longchamps, Mazas, and myself over to where he's standing with the motorcycle driver. "You're a dignified crew." He reaches out to shake our hands. "Godspeed." His bloodshot eyes appear heavy with tears. Yet he doesn't shed a drop; he just returns to the warehouse and addresses the soldiers waiting.

"There are plenty of places to find a truck," I tell Mazas as we hurry to the waiting convoy. "There's got to be more in Sarrebourg or one of the surrounding farms."

He nods and makes a clicking noise but doesn't respond. I board the rear Renault and the flatbed rumbles as the engine is put into gear. We move out. There are twenty of us in the truck, and unlike the military Renaults, no canvas cloth covers the top but rather a bare, metal frame. We approach the main highway and then come to a dead halt. I look out from the side at the lead Citroen and the impenetrable line of vehicles the small car is trying to merge into.

Mazas sits beside me, also craning his head out to see. "This is madness."

Trucks and cars of every make and model are jammed bumper to bumper. Even bicycles and motorcycles have difficulty weaving through, yet those on horseback seem to be navigating better. The roar of engines drowns out conversations, and our faces stare forward in this sea of vehicles.

Ten minutes pass, and everyone chain-smokes cigarettes. I had to part with my beloved record player. I wonder if one of the men left behind will take it despite being ordered to leave all unnecessary items. Probably not. If the Germans reach Sarrebourg, it might be commandeered by a member of the SS. What a pity. Better to have been destroyed, tossed in the fire with the ledgers.

Finally, the Citroen merges into the traffic, and the first truck manages to snake along behind. We wait, and the second truck makes it onto the road, then ours a short time later. We are all together now, separated, but we can see one another's truck, and the motorcycle beside the lead Renault keeps watch of us all.

***

We go so slowly that soon half an hour passes, and then an hour. Without traffic, we would have arrived in Saverne by now. But at least we managed to get all our vehicles together in a line at the eastern turnoff. I close my eyes, but sleep is impossible. The truck bed bucks and vibrates. My eyes open out of a semiconscious state, blinking wearily at a dim evening.

"What's going on?" I ask Mazas as we park on the side of the road.

The tip of his cigarette illuminates. "Not sure. The Citroen motioned for us to pull over."

"Where's the motorcycle?" I look out the window, but all I can see is the spectral red glare of taillights mirroring off the roadway.

"Gone."

"Gone?"

The glow of his cigarette goes back and forth as he shakes his head, half his face visible in a crescent light. "Didn't see it go, but it's gone. Took off."

Mazas opens his door to step out, and I do the same. It feels good to stand. I look around; half the men sleep or close their eyes while others smoke. I open a can of sardines and share them with Mazas, both of us using our fingers to pull the greasy little fish from confinement.

After I toss the empty tin and pull a cigarette from the pack with my teeth, I hear Longchamps. "Mazas! Zenner!"

"Coming," I say, and the men part for us to pass. Longchamps is bathed in red from the sea of taillights, and I view well past him that the road ahead ends at a cross-section, with our route going straight and over a bridge … only, the bridge is not there.

"It's blown," Longchamps says, scratching his chin.

"Who destroyed it?" Mazas asks. "The Germans?"

Longchamps shakes his head. "There's no indication the Wehrmacht has reached this far South. It was either the French army or people in an opposing town to slow the Germans' advance."

We're quiet as a map is produced. Ross, driving the lead truck, and Brissanet, manning the second, arrive. We huddle near a headlight as

Longchamps runs a finger over the paper, finding our location. Voulard emerges from the shadows, his girth as wide as two men. He had been driving the Citroen. "What's the plan?" he asks.

"We're figuring that out," Mazas answers.

"All right," Longchamps says. "We're right …"—his finger stops—"here."

The map displays the road ahead, turning left and right before the bridge.

"The next bridge is thirty kilometers south." Longchamps points.

"It will take forever to get there," Voulard says.

"We should take into account that we have no way of knowing if that bridge is also blown," Mazas adds.

Longchamps nods and lights a cigarette. "Agreed."

We study the map but can't find a better route to Saverne.

After a pause, Longchamps says, "South then. We don't go to Saverne." He exhales a cloud of smoke and continues, "Lieutenant Serre gave us orders to navigate new paths if necessary."

"It appears it's necessary," Voulard says.

"So …" Longchamps pauses, then continues, "Epinal." He points to a black dot on the map. "It's well over a hundred kilometers away, but with any luck, the traffic will loosen once we're distanced from the bridge. If we progress, we'll continue past Epinal and to Dijon."

We all agree and study the route. The men on the trucks have fifteen minutes to stretch their legs. I sit in the passenger seat beside Mazas, who takes the next shift, so Longchamps can navigate from the lead Citroen. The men are told to regroup, and the ones napping on the soft grass on the shoulder of the road stir. I close my eyes, but sleep remains distant.

The fuel is replenished from large vats brought along, and the trucks rumble to life. I drift in and out of sleep, with Mazas occasionally rousing me to ask where we might be. It's too dark to see road signs, so I guess.

"What time is it?" he asks, now several hours behind the wheel.

"About five." I scratch my cheek, stubble grinding against my fingertips.

"Jesus. We've been traveling for, what … ten hours? How far have we gone?"

"Maybe a hundred kilometers. A little less."

We are quiet for a long stretch, chain-smoking cigarettes. My eyes are dry and sore, and I wonder how Mazas is feeling, but I don't ask. He'll say, "I'm fine," even if he's not.

The sky lightens, and the crush of vehicles becomes visible. We are going at a crawl, but at least we're moving. A horse-drawn carriage is up ahead, and to my right is a car with two barrels of wine strapped to the top. Another small truck has mattresses in the back, and a line of people walk on the side of the road, sometimes moving quicker than the vehicles. Men and women of all ages carry suitcases and packages, some pushing baby carriages.

"This is not the France I want to remember," I tell Mazas.

"France is not a memory. It hasn't fallen."

I don't respond.

A sign ahead catches my eye. "There. You see it?" I squint.

Mazas leans forward. Soon, I can make out the words. "Darney, it says. Two kilometers. We've passed Epinal," I say happily. "Dijon is what …" I study the map. "A hundred and fifty or so kilometers away."

Mazas smiles. Dijon is well fortified, much more so than Saverne, and far from the fighting in the north. We will be safe there. I light two cigarettes, pass one to Mazas, and go through my backpack for a loaf of bread. Traffic creeps along, but we are happy to be moving at all. Half an hour passes when another road sign appears, reading *Bourbonne-les-Bains*. The road goes straight across the sleepy little town, and aside from the convoy of people on foot, I don't see inhabitants in the homes or businesses. It's maybe nine in the morning, and nobody is going to work, shopping for groceries, or talking on the sidewalks.

We pass a roundabout with a fountain in the center, the water still. A noise pierces the air just as we exit the town, so loud my eardrums vibrate. The procession of vehicles comes to an abrupt halt, and doors fly open. Mazas doesn't have to say it, but he does anyway: "Air raid!"

I open the door and see the men jumping out of the truck behind me.

"Here!" Longchamps yells to no one in particular but more to the civilians. "Under the trees!"

People run in every direction. Some lie on their stomachs in the middle of cow pastures, and others hide under cars. Horses whiny and snort. Most of our entourage gathers at the base of a cluster of trees, and we wait, scanning the horizon for the sight and sounds of the Luftwaffe and any indication of fire or bombs being dropped. My heart thumps against my uniform as if it might explode from my chest like a hand grenade.

The shrill siren mixes with the screaming from the civilians and the cries of the children, and I'm not sure which is a worse uproar. Faces look to us and other soldiers traveling in the gridlock. Still, we can offer nothing regarding safety except to shout, "Get down! Get down!"

A few minutes pass, though it feels like hours when the sirens stop, yet my ears still ring. We wait, scanning the sky. Slowly, people stand, emerge from trees and thickets, searching the heavens. They return to their vehicles and carriages, and soon, everyone is hurrying to leave this place.

It takes a while for the congestion to move, and with it comes terrible anxiety. Soldiers from the front line, who I've spoken to in the past, told me that Luftwaffe planes will be heard before bombs are dropped. Still, I scan the sky, waiting for explosions. Once the truck is put into drive and we move, my uniform is soaked with perspiration.

I light a cigarette with shaky hands and say, "You think the Luftwaffe is close enough to trigger air raid sirens?"

"No." Mazas shakes his head and lights his own cigarette. "Faulty nerves is all. Someone saw a flock of birds or something."

I'm not so sure. The congestion continues, and I'm relieved when Bourbonne-les-Bains disappears from the rearview mirror.

"Hey," Mazas says, pointing ahead. "You see that?"

I look up. There's movement on the opposite lane, a lone car traveling toward us. "We need to tell them to turn around," I say.

Mazas rolls down his window and sticks his head out, but when they near, the other driver yells in a panic, "Turn around! Wrong way!" A truck appears behind the lead car, then another, and more. People from our line of traffic shout warnings to them, and we are given warnings in return.

"Go back!" they say in urgency. "The Germans are in Dijon!"

Chapter Four
Saturday, 15 June, 1940

The village to our right burns. Blades of fire erupt from ruined buildings, cutting away the dark. The road is desperate, with craters large enough to stand in. I walk in front of the truck with others, shouting orders to Mazas where and when to turn to avoid more considerable wreckage. All the vehicles keep their headlights off to avoid being sighted by the Luftwaffe high up in the black sky, and it's a strange, dark procession. We slept on comfortable mattresses and cots a few days ago, only to find apocalypse tonight.

We wasted valuable time retracing a similar route back north until we conferred and settled on a course to Vesoul. With the German border a little over a hundred kilometers east, and the north and west quickly falling, we have no choice but to travel south. The Wehrmacht is a hammer and Germany the anvil, with our caravan the ember iron between the two, about to be struck.

A motorcycle snakes around our truck's front, and the driver shouts, "Halt!" The firelight from the village illuminates his officer insignia, belonging to the National Gendarmerie. The trucks stop and nudge as close to the rocky shoulder as possible, and the officer motions for a small car to pass. He tells me, "We're going ahead to clear the traffic." Mazas leans out from the open window to hear what the man says. We wait until the officer leaves, and I return to the passenger seat.

"He's lying," I say to Mazas.

"Probably," Mazas responds and navigates back onto the road.

We continue for a while, and then traffic comes to a complete stop. We can't see past the line of vehicles stuck in the procession, so I tell Mazas that I will be right back and leave to walk along the side of the road. I hadn't gone far before seeing a dozen abandoned vehicles parked haphazardly along the pavement. It's difficult to see in the dark, but several trucks crashed together, and the passengers fled. The officer on the motorcycle is nowhere to be seen. People are attempting to push the damaged vehicles aside, with little progress. I return to our convoy and point to the first ten soldiers in the back of the lead truck. "On me," I tell them, and we return to the pile-up and heave the abandoned vehicles to open a lane.

The gridlock loosens and crawls over the rough and broken ground. I stay outside, leading Mazas around the scattered glass and twisted scrapes from the crash. When the traffic picks up speed, I return to the passenger seat, and Longchamps takes over driving. Seeing the road ahead is difficult, so I tell Longchamps, "I have an idea," and explain what I'm thinking.

"Okay," he says. "It's worth a try. I can barely see the car bumper ahead." We're going slow enough that Longchamps doesn't have to come to a complete stop as I pull myself out the open window and climb onto the roof. I shine my almost dead flashlight in short intervals when the road bends and catch a glimmer of a sign stating, *Vesoul, thirteen kilometers*. We're close.

Soon after, another sign reads, *Entering Port-sur-Saône*. A few homes appear tucked in the countryside: ashen buildings with red tiled roofs and dilapidated barns. As we near the town center, the buildings have grown numerous until the businesses have been clustered. It is late, and no lights emerge behind closed curtains or from the narrow windows of the unassuming cathedral.

We are going downhill at a better speed than most of our travels, at almost a free roll. All at once, the sky lights up in a blinding strobe of white, and the earth trembles with a terrible explosion. The roar is thunderous. I catch myself before falling off the truck's roof as a wave of blistering heat surges over my body.

"Holy hell!" I shout. My own words muted against the ringing in my eardrums.

A pillar of fire erupts before us as the bridge is blown to rubble, with less than a dozen vehicles separating us from the inferno. The traffic comes to a fast halt, and I crash forward onto the hood. Rocks rain down, plunking against the metal of the truck and striking the exposed soldiers and civilians.

I slide off the hood and scramble to the passenger side door.

"What the fuck happened!" Longchamps shouts.

"They blew the bridge!" I yell back, although I'm aware his question is rhetorical. "Why was it blown?"

Longchamps doesn't answer, but when we hear screaming near the riverbank, he says, "Come on," and opens his door. We get out as the soldiers jump from the flat tops and join the mass converging at the water's edge. Morning is turning the sky a milky blue. Still, there is such a dense fog coming off the Saône River and mixing with the smoke that it's difficult to see past the opposite shoreline. A short portion of the bridge juts out over the steady rapids below, ending in a jagged roadway.

"Was anyone on the bridge when it blew?" I ask no one in particular. There is no response, but there must have been since the lead truck at the edge of the pavement was scorched from the blast. The driver is being tended to, with weltering burns on his arms and face. Smoke heaves from the homes bordering the bridge, and firelight dances from rooftops and shoots from windows.

There is no way to know who blew the bridge, but by the lack of German soldiers, it's safe to say that the Wehrmacht is not at fault.

"It was probably someone in the procession," Longchamps whispers. "One of the cars got over the bridge and blew it to stop the Germans from pursuing."

I'm enraged to think that one of us, someone stuck in the same traffic jam, had lit the fuse. But we will never know.

I turn to see Longchamps and Mazas staring at the convoy behind us. As far as the horizon is long, both lanes are lined with thousands of vehicles. The rush of people toward the shoreline becomes thicker as more and more people abandon their cars and trucks. Fearful faces: children, mothers and fathers clutching wailing babies, carrying suitcases and strollers. A man passes holding a birdcage, the bird inside squawking a melodic shriek and shaking loose, soft, fluffy feathers as it's roughed about. Dogs weave through the crowd, and barks and growls cut through the chatter.

"We have to get out of here," Longchamps says.

"How are we supposed to do that?" Mazas replies. "There's no way for us to turn the trucks around. And even if we could, where will we go?"

"We leave the trucks and find a way across the river."

The Saône River, flowing before us in all its glory, and the boulders of the destroyed bridge swallowed up in its lapping tide. We must cross it.

Chapter Five
Sunday, 16 June, 1940

We should have traveled between six hundred to eight hundred kilometers in two days. Instead, as morning arises on the third day, we are roughly two hundred kilometers from our starting point. What did we bring when we left that warehouse with every conceivable good? More cigarettes than a platoon could smoke in a lifetime, yet a mere quantity of food to last three days. What were we thinking?

Our trucks are stuck in gridlock, along with hundreds, perhaps thousands of other vehicles leading into Port-sur-Saône. I take a quick inventory before heading out and worry about our rations. Longchamps tells us to pack only what we need: food and water, extra clothing, blankets, two bottles of champagne per man, and however many packs of cigarettes we can carry. Goodbye, typewriter.

"We're going to follow the riverbank," Longchamps shouts to the company as we ready our bags. "There's rumor among the people that army engineers have constructed a bridge less than a kilometer upstream."

Before leaving, we consolidate all the essential documents and ledgers taken from the warehouse, stacking the boxes atop the other on the side of the road. They were supposed to be given to command when and if we arrived there. Mazas splashes gasoline over the pile from a canister, and I drop a match. Flames engulf them, and we walk off as the pages burn. I turn back to catch a glimpse of the dancing fire, ash dancing away, and feel that not only is my hard work being destroyed, but my life as I knew it is being erased in the glowing embers.

I stay close to Longchamps as he leads the company. A man runs past me, bumping my shoulder. The closer we get to the bridge, the more the civilians panic. Mothers hold crying children; men shout at one another. It's a strange noise, listening to the mass of people speaking, yelling, sobbing, all at once.

"Keep going," Longchamps shouts to the gathering.

We walk down a grassy embankment to reach the shoreline. Behind, a drove of people follow our lead. Far up on the hill, by the congested roadway, a thick black smoke snakes the heavens and darkens the dawn.

Our company helps civilians by holding suitcases or the arms of the elderly faltering on the soft soil. I turn to a woman beside me, with a baby in one arm and struggling to push a carriage containing another child with the other. A wheel gets stuck, and she strains to release it. The women in the group are far quieter than the men and elderly, especially the ones with children.

"You have to leave the carriage," I tell the woman.

She looks at me with stark brown eyes. Her mouth begins to form words, and I see her cheeks glisten with wet tears as her bottom lip wavers. How lucky I am to not have the burden of a child and how dreadful it must be for the people who do. Ever since I can remember, I yearned for the love of a wife and a family to call my own. I idealized the happy couples walking arm-in-arm along the Parisian avenues and imagined their conversations at cafés. I was jealous of men my age pushing strollers and pointing out the beautiful sculptures spread throughout the city to the wonderous gaze of their toddlers. But now, I am relieved not to have the responsibility.

"Here," I say and offer to hold her child. She's reluctant but knows that the carriage cannot go further. She hands me the baby, who weighs no more than the thin blanket nuzzled around its body. The child wails, tears streaking down its tiny cheeks, and I clutch it tight to my chest.

"Is it a girl?" I ask as the mother leans into the carriage to remove the other child.

"Yes," she replies.

As we move on, more possessions are being abandoned, mainly bicycles and suitcases. When we near the second bridge, the group groans in dismay.

"It's blown," Mazas mutters.

The baby squirms, yearning for her mother.

"There's another way across," a middle-aged man in uniform says, approaching through the crowd. "I've traveled through Port-sur-Saône many times. There is a path ahead if we continue along the bank. At the end is a lock. We can cross there."

An explosion from where we'd left the vehicles causes everyone to recoil, and many scream. Another explosion follows, and oily smoke fills the distant sky. I stare, mesmerized. The man I'd seen earlier holding the birdcage is beside me, still clutching the wire enclosure. The bright, tiny bird flutters within.

"It must be the gas tanks," Mazas says. "The fire spread. The vehicles have caught flame."

"All right," Longchamps tells the crowd. "Let's find the path." He turns and takes up the trail, following the middle-aged soldier. All eyes have fallen upon us to lead this burden.

The baby in my arms is howling and sometimes seems unable to breathe when inhaling. The mother thanks me and takes her child back, holding one in each arm, hushing them as tears drop from her eyes and onto their foreheads. Mazas leans close to my ear and says, "This better not be a dead end." I try not to think about it as we trample through brush. Every time a child or adult wails or shrieks in fear, a red-hot blade of anxiety pierces my heart.

The middle-aged soldier says, "This is it," and points. "The lock is up there."

The press of the crowd grows tight as a tall bulkhead comes into view. Ghostly fingers of thick fog creep over the top from the river, yet the wall is too tall to see the water beyond.

"It must be over two meters high," Longchamps says. "Brissanet, Batist, Voulard—all of you—collect those stones." He points to the side of the path, and I notice his finger is shaking.

We go to a line of trees and begin prying up stones the size of small boulders and bringing them to the bulkhead's base to act as steps. Already, people are scrambling to get on top. Men push women and the elderly out of their way, and women nudge others with suitcases and shoulders. Longchamps shouts, "Wait your turn!" to little avail.

Half of our company makes it to the top, and they reach down to assist others. I stay at the bottom with Longchamps, Mazas, and Brissanet, pushing and shoving people to reach the ledge. Many men don't need to use the steps, but women carrying babies, the elderly, and many children cannot make it over, even with the steps. Boots trample me as I am used as a ladder, and I'm shoved against the wall. "Bastard!" I shout to a man who pushes others aside and presses his muddy shoes against my thigh to get ahold of the rim.

A woman holds out a baby for me to take, shouting through her tears, "Save my baby!" It's a familiar scream, along with, "Save my mother! Save my sister!" A man with a bicycle nearly knocks her and her baby over. Mazas grabs the bike as the man attempts to push it atop the wall. "What's wrong with you!" Mazas shouts and throws the bicycle aside. He squares up and throws three quick punches. They all land, and the man stumbles backward, not issuing a word in reply or a punch thrown back. He vanishes into the crowd, holding his nose.

The congestion thins as more and more people get up and over the wall. Longchamps tells Mazas and Brissanet to hoist themselves up to help the assembly cross the lock. There are three people left at the bottom now. Two manage to get themselves up using the stone steps, and the last is a frail, elderly lady with a cane. She is tiny and delicate, but I fear I've grown weak after helping so many people. She hobbles over, and I say, "Come on now, hurry!"

Instant regret hits me for scolding her, but my muscles are trembling with fatigue, and I want to get over the wall myself and to safety. The lady says, "My right knee is partially paralyzed. Please, my legs are in a lot of pain. Be careful. Please."

I begin to lift her, but my arms and legs ache. Longchamps lies down on the top of the wall, trying to clasp her outstretched arm, but can't get a good grip. I tell her to stand with her back against the wall, and I grab either side of her torso, feel her frail ribcage in my hands as I strain to push her up. The fabric of her long gown is slippery. Two people come running out from the brush, both men. I shout to them, "Help us, please!" but they ignore my pleading and ascend the stone steps—the exact steps I dragged to that spot— and hoist themselves up and disappear.

Longchamps scowls, "Cowards!" He still can't get a hold of her, and I can't push her any higher, so he jumps down, and we both clutch the lady and shove.

She yells, "My legs! My legs!" but we don't stop, we can't stop, we have to get her up. Either that or leave her behind. When she is on top and rolls away from the edge, I hoist myself up and reach down for Longchamps' hand. Sweat stings my eyes as he makes it up, and we both collapse on our backs, out of breath and fatigued. The old lady sits beside us, crying with her hands over her face, and I begin to cry too, and so does Longchamps. The sobbing of one terrified woman is far worse than the collective shrieking from the group. When I look down at the landing, a solitary birdcage is left behind. The door open, loose feathers escaping in the wind.

Chapter Six
Chasing a Train

The middle-aged soldier who helped us find the boat lock introduces himself as Seguin. He is a sergeant who lost his company when they fled Dijon. "I didn't see any fighting," he tells us. "During the last war, I fought in Verdun. They stationed me as an ambulance driver in this new war due to my knee here." He points to his leg and bends it halfway before it stops. "I encountered a rather large Hun in a trench, and he stuck me in the leg and right here." Seguin points to his side. "My knee never healed proper. But it took me away from the fighting in Verdun."

"What happened to the German?" Mazas asks.

"Only one of us left the trench, crawling or otherwise."

We don't instruct the civilians to follow us, but many do. After a quick deliberation and a few sips from our canteens, we decided to follow a set of train tracks a half kilometer away.

"If I'm right," Seguin tells us, "the station is south of the heart of Vesoul."

"What's the likelihood of a train being at the station?" I ask.

"Slim."

We pack our canteens and shoulder our backpacks. My body aches from the exertion by the waterside, but the initial walk is easy. As we near the tracks, the path becomes riddled with rocks and shallow holes. All the men in the company help the civilians, even Voulard, who is obese and always out of breath, and Piffet, who is frail. Longchamps hoists a girl, perhaps five, onto his shoulders, and she slumps forward, resting her cheek against the top of his head. Her little eyes are closed, and her chest extends with deep breaths of slumber against the back of his neck. With all of the children cared for, I help an older gentleman with a suitcase.

"Wait." Longchamps tries not to move his head, disturbing the child from her dreams. "Did you hear that?"

Nobody stops walking, but as we quiet down and listen, the unmistakable rumble of engines cuts above the noise of boots against gravel. We walk faster, even the elderly, and when we turn a bend, buildings bordering a town come into view. We are quick across the streets and avenues, seeing nobody until we enter a plaza with a dry fountain in the center. Six military convoys are parked alongside one another. A soldier yells as he sees us, "We don't have room!" He waves his hands dismissively before him, anxious the mob will overcome him, then relents, "Women and children only!"

Longchamps hands the sleepy child back to her mother and steps aside as the few who can fit scuttle aboard the back of the trucks. When it's full, more women and children grab onto the sides and climb atop the canvas awnings. Some cry, waving farewell to their sobbing fathers who have no choice but to stay behind.

"The rest of you better hurry," the soldier tells us. "There's a train at the station less than a kilometer away. It might have departed already. The Germans have crossed Port-sur-Saône." The man wrinkles his mustache and leaves to the passenger door. The trucks are put in gear and rumble out from the plaza.

A hundred or so of us are left, many crying in fear and loss, and Longchamps says, "Come on, let's go."

I don't look behind to see if the civilians follow, but I know they do. There is nowhere to go. If it's true that the Wehrmacht has passed Port-sur-Saône, they could be in this nameless town any moment.

Back on the tracks, we sprint until we see a small station with an idling locomotive parked before it. A conductor spies us from the platform and panics at seeing our swarm emerging from the brush. Then he composes himself and shouts with his hands cupping his mouth to amplify his voice, "Hurry up!"

"What luck!" Mazas says, and we all run as fast as we can. Our company is well ahead of the civilians, except those helping the others, and Voulard and Piffet, who are wheezing in the rear.

As we near, we see three trains waiting, not one. The first in line is a passenger train, which the conductor motions the civilians toward. The middle is a Red Cross wagon, and the rear train is for cargo, tanks, artillery, and large munitions. Brissanet is first to the cargo train, and I follow behind, with Chanal close at my heels. Voulard is the last to arrive, and everyone collapses on their backs, taking in lungfuls of air. Poor Voulard can't recover enough oxygen, and his complexion is a deep crimson. After a moment, no one else from the company arrives. I peek outside. The trains aren't moving, so I hop down and see Longchamps craning from the passenger train.

"Come on!" he shouts. "Keep together!"

We all hear Longchamps and begin to run to the passenger train. We make it to the wagon's rear as the wheels glide forward. Brissanet is behind me, and so is Chanal. It's as if I cannot get enough air into my lungs, and my head is dizzy. But Voulard is still running, stumbling over stones and rough ground, and it looks as if he might topple over.

"Christ," I mutter and sprint to him. He goes a little faster after I take his backpack and grab his arm, pulling him forward. "Come on!" I shout. The poor guy can't reply. But we make it to the handrails as the train quickens and pull ourselves on board, weary and beaten. Voulard holds his chest and says, "I-I'm s-sorry."

I pat him on the knee as we sit across from each other and smile. "You made it. We all made it."

Once we catch our breaths, I get to my feet and extend a hand to help him. The train car is packed with rail workers, every seat is taken, and the aisle is crammed. Hundreds of terrified faces, fear-struck eyes. Expressions convey uncertainty over whether they will make it home, if their loved ones are safe, and if their mothers, fathers, wives, and children will be found once the train arrives at a secure terminal.

"Zenner, Voulard," I hear and see Longchamps at the far end of the cabin, along with Mazas and a dozen of our company. They stand beside a washroom, and Ross steps out with his face still dripping water. They're sharing bottles of champagne, and when I'm close enough, Longchamps hands me a bottle. The rush of bubbles on my tongue feels incredible and warms my stomach. "We're missing five from our unit," he says. "I think they boarded the Red Cross train. Brissanet, do a head count; find who's not here."

Brissanet nods and stands, pulling out a pad and pencil, and starts writing the names of the men from our unit as he looks us over.

Longchamps turns to an older man wearing coveralls whom he was speaking to prior. The man's wrinkled face is soot-covered, as is our own. Longchamps says, "Tell them what you just told me."

The man looks at Voulard and myself, and I pass him the champagne. He takes a swig and issues an audible sigh of pleasure. Then he says, "Paris has fallen."

This is not surprising. It shouldn't be surprising. Yet the words make the champagne sour in my stomach.

"I heard it on the radio this morning," the man continues. "The Wehrmacht walked in without a fight. There's talk among the workers that negotiations are underway to make an accord with Germany, but I don't know the details. France, it appears, is falling."

"I'm going to be sick," Voulard says.

"Tell them what else you told me," Longchamps says.

"Well," the man pauses to take another swig, then continues, "they're not being too kind to French military, surrendering or otherwise. There are reports of the Wehrmacht performing executions on the spot. Making examples of soldiers. Hanging them from trees. Shooting them in the head, cutting throats. All without consequence."

Longchamps turns to our unit. "We need to continue south. Paris must have fallen before Dijon. And if it's true that they're outside of Port-sur-Saône, they're making fast progress. Once we pass Besancon, we will be safe and can renegotiate a path. The Germans won't rush into the countryside with cities still in their paths."

The washroom door opens, and Weber steps out. I turn from the rail worker and go inside. No words can convey my disgust knowing German boots are trampling Paris avenues. The water runs cold from the faucet, and it feels marvelous washed over my face. Brown water swirls down the drain, and I look in the mirror and try to decipher the discorded thoughts of the man staring back at me. Eyes red, underlined in dark circles. A scrape on my chin. Springy hair, uncombed. I remove my shaving kit, but realize I left my soap behind in the truck. Nonetheless, I drag the sharp blade over my wet skin.

Of course, we know the Germans have perhaps the most powerful single force in the world—but against the allied French and English? The Nazis should have been suppressed when they first stepped foot on foreign land. They should have been pushed back to Berlin, stripped of power. How could we let them rise again? Where are the Americans? They fought in the last war and lost many lives. Do they think they're safe from Germany's wrath? If we made a united front at the beginning, Hitler would be hanging from a tree, his officers jailed …

… this way of thinking does no good. The *whys* and *hows*, the constant stream of questions going through everyone's mind and discussed at length in private and public, do nothing to solve problems. They do nothing to make sense of the French government's inactions and the stupidity of not extending the Maginot Line across the Belgian border.

The reflection looking back, the blue eyes cast red, tell the tale of a tired man who should not dwell in the *hows* and *whys*. Focusing on the current ordeal is essential. Where are we going? What will we do once we get there? The reflection staring back registers that the worst is still to come.

Chapter Seven
Vesoul

The train goes at a crawl for many kilometers and then halts. Minutes pass, then more minutes, and we've been stationary for half an hour. I see from out the window some of the rail workers gathered outside, smoking cigarettes and sharing bottles of drink, so I say to Mazas, "Maybe we should look for Weber and the others?" He agrees, and we squeeze through the tight cabin until we're outside.

At the far length of the passenger track, close to the Red Cross car, we see Weber and four others walking our way. Mazas calls them over.

"Did everyone make it?" Weber asks.

"Yes," Mazas tells him.

We speak to some rail workers on the way back, exchanging cigarettes and rumors. They're wearier than us Terrified. Soldiers have been away from our homes and families for months, but many of the rail workers were torn away from their homes hours ago, separated from their parents, wives, and children. They don't know if they'll ever return.

My parents and family are well away from the fighting, at least for now. As a teenager, I couldn't wait until I was old enough to move off the farm, go to Paris, be among art and history, people and adventure. Be rid of sheep and chickens, the barnyard odor of stale hay and manure. When I packed my bags to leave, my stepfather only requested that I take a profession and work under my uncle at his bakery in Paris. It was an easy request to fill. As soon as I arrived in that great city, I knew I was home. My uncle rented me an apartment he owns, six floors above the bakery. But now, I'm glad my mother and stepfather never moved to Paris. They are safe in the fields of Charolles, far enough from the city.

My parents may not yet know that Paris has fallen. Their old radio never picked up a clear signal to begin with. I doubt they purchased a new one. They shouldn't know the scope of France's quick decline. My mother shouldn't worry about my safety. Her attention is needed in the fields, tending to their much-needed food sources. Her hands have spent so many years toiling in the soil that her fingers resemble the twisted root vegetables she pulls. And with my stepfather's eyesight faltering, so much rests on her shoulders.

Yes, I'd rather them stay in the dark. If at least for my own mental stability.

Our unit gathers in the same cabin, and we take inventory of our little food. I'm stacking pouches of stale, wrapped biscuits, when the train crawls forward. For several kilometers, we stop and go. For one particularly long halt, we are in a tunnel, and it is pitch black. Then, just as my eyes become accustomed, we lurch onward.

"What time is it?" Mazas asks, rubbing his wrist where his watch should be.

"A little after nine," I say. "Where's your watch?"

"Left it in the warehouse, I think. Did I have it in the truck?"

I shrug.

Everyone on the train has either found a seat or sits on the aisle, and most of our company sleeps. We've grown accustomed to the constant stops, so when the train comes to a halt, everyone remains where they are in contemplation.

The cabin door is flung open, and a man wearing a Red Cross on his sleeve bursts in. "Get out!" he screams, stepping over sleeping bodies, stumbling over others, shaking sleeping shoulders. "Planes are coming! Everyone, get out!" Sure enough, the faint groaning of plane engines can be heard.

The cabin erupts in screams and panic. "Christ," Longchamps says as he's pushed along with the mass of bodies. For a moment, the throng is stuck at the doorway, people clutching suitcases and small children, making a corkscrew at the doorframe. But it bursts free like the bubbles of champagne, and people flood outside, falling on top of each other. I follow a group of rail workers to an open field and dive into the tall grass. A lone mother screams beside me, her face contorted by fear and wet with tears. I take her child without asking and cover its little sobbing body with my own. The mother curls beside me, her head under my shoulder, howling louder than the child. I look to my other side and see Brissanet shielding a different child and Longchamps lying over an elderly couple.

The droning grows louder, and a squadron crosses far overhead. A shadowy pack of murderous crows against the pale morning sky, flying low and right above us. A collective scream erupts as the first explosion rips across the valley, followed by a steady succession. Vesoul is being bombed. Pillars of black smoke dart into the sky and fill the horizon. After the planes pass and the droning of their engines lessens, someone shouts, "The trains are moving!"

The crowd is fast to their feet, and I hand the child back to its mother. I have no idea if it is a boy or a girl, and I don't ask. As usual, the men are far louder and more panicked than the women, and the soldiers are calmest.

The train barely moves as everyone gets on board, but nobody sits or lies in the aisles this time. Everyone is sweating, smoking cigarettes, and speaking in a tumult of noise. We haven't traveled for more than half a kilometer when the train stops again, and the low rumbling of plane engines returns.

"Mazas!" I shout above the uproar as we are shoved toward the door. He hears me, and I point to a mother holding a child near him, being smothered by the throng. Mazas resists the press of the crowd so that she and her infant can move forward. Outside, a terrible explosion bursts so loud that the train rocks on the tracks. When I enter the doorway, a blaze of hot wind greets me, and dancing firelight flashes close.

Everyone runs, screaming, as more planes come into view, and fall to their stomachs or continue running into the shadows. The squadron flies low toward Vesoul, but three break off their approach and veer in our direction. Voices shout, "Get down! Get down!" Dozens of explosions send discord rocketing in every which way, and I cover my ears against painful vibrations. White flashes are blinding, and hot gusts blanket the field. I shout to Voulard, "What are they targeting?" but he doesn't respond.

The detonations cease, and the planes turn toward Vesoul until they disappear into the pillars of black smoke pouring from the city. One by one, people stand and look at the skyline. The day is dawning a pale gray through cracks in the oily smoke, with bright shades of oranges and reds from the fire. One of the trains has been destroyed, blown to twisted, blackened scraps, the railway in complete disarray, and in the distance, Vesoul burns. "It's the ammunition car," someone says. "The damn Luftwaffe blew up the ammunition car!"

"Jesus," I say to Voulard. "We were on that train at the station."

He doesn't respond, but the look on his face gives away his realization that we escaped death by chance alone. Then he says, "Whatever you've been writing in your journal, the story would have ended." He looks past me. "The company is gathering past the lead train."

I turn to see Longchamps and Mazas motioning everyone together. "Hurry!" Longchamps waves us over. "Let's go!"

Voulard and I shoulder our backpacks and catch up. Some civilians join, and we hurry along the tracks. "First the trucks and now this," Brissanet says, pointing his thumb behind us.

Longchamps takes a headcount as we move. "We've lost some," he says, but nobody stops. "They might have run off, but let's hope they're up ahead."

Soon, a road is visible alongside the tracks. Army trucks drive fast away from the burning city. One stops and a young soldier sticks his head out the open window. "They're bombing Vesoul!" he shouts.

"We know!" Mazas responds. Explosions still sound in the distance, along with the detonation of antivehicle guns and munitions.

"They've crossed Port-sur-Saône. You all better move!" With that, he disappears back inside the vehicle.

"We were in Port-sur-Saône yesterday," Brissanet tells me. "We watched the sunrise over the water, and now the Germans have crossed the river."

"How did they cross so fast?"

"What does it matter?" Brissanet asks. "They've crossed. How the hell are we supposed to outrun the goddamn Wehrmacht?"

Longchamps cuts in, "They're not following us, for one. They'll slow their advance at Besancon. I can't imagine them progressing at their current pace without pause in the major cities."

Brissanet shrugs. "There's a lot of things I can't imagine. How they took Paris, for one. Walked right in ..." He spits to his side. "Vermin, all of them. We should have wiped the entire German race off the map when we had the chance after the last war."

We move off the tracks and onto the road. The pavement radiates heat upward like a frying pan from the morning sunshine. A few homes line the side of the avenue as we enter a village, and I eye a low stone structure in a plaza ahead. "Look there." I point. "There's a fountain."

We circle the small fountain, taking turns to dip in our hands and drink the cool water. Mazas cleans his face, and many do the same. Mothers fill their palms for their children to drink, and soldiers replenish their canteens, offering them out to the crowd. More vehicles speed by, and Longchamps and Mazas wave them down.

"Cowards!" Longchamps shouts as they quicken.

Finally, two trucks stop. "We have room," the driver says. "Women and children first."

We help the women and children board the trucks and then the males. They manage to get all of them on board, and the vehicles are as packed as possible. Without another word, the trucks depart.

We again fill our canteens, and Longchamps says, "There are eighteen of us. Let's hope the others are ahead or got away from the trains safely." He kneels next to the fountain and again washes his face and head. Hearing Longchamps sigh as the cold water washes over his hair and seeing his eyes close for a moment, I feel the strain he is enduring. The man never asked to be in charge; he was ordered to assume the position. Although he is our leader, we are all friends, and there is little military formality when speaking to each other. I doubt Lieutenant Serre would be leading us any better.

Longchamps stands and brushes water from his face. His eyes are open, and his expression returns to its usual stern demeanor. "Get your gear," he tells the group. "Move out."

Chapter Eight
Inventory

We travel on the road for hours, and the Luftwaffe's rumbling engines dissipate as we make distance. Now that the civilians are all gone, we're making fast progress. As evening arrives, a small, deserted town appears on our path, and we inspect the homes and buildings for any indication of life.

"Up there." Longchamps points to a door left ajar.

It's evening as we enter an office building and inspect each room. There are plenty of books, ledgers, and desks, but no food. We set up for the night, all finding some ground and taking turns keeping watch. Sleep seems impossible, but exhaustion extends a heavy blanket over us all, and soon, snoring bellows from the silence. The only light comes from matches being struck to light cigarettes, casting the faces of the smokers in crescent illumination.

At some point, my mind swims to a dark and dreamless slumber. The sun is barely up when Longchamps says, "Let's move out. We should stay off the road."

Everyone is eager to make headway. My eyes are bleary as I roll my blanket and shoulder my gear.

Outside, we listen to the wind for the indication of engines but don't hear anything, so we hasten to the countryside. Acres of cow pastures and grape orchards stretch in every direction across a limitless horizon. Longchamps leads us up a slight incline and shouts from the top, "Careful ahead." The land has been bombed, with gaping hollows where vining plants had been growing. Whole cherry trees burst into splinters.

"It's damn hot out," Mazas says.

We both look back at the men and scan their faces. Their eyes are cast to the ground, cheeks red, dripping perspiration. It's rough terrain, and minding the craters and blown-about rocks is a chore. "Let's take a break up there." Mazas points to a line of trees in the distance.

"Agreed," Longchamps says, and the men behind voice their approval.

We stumble over rocks and holes to reach the treeline, and Longchamps says, "Careful not to twist an ankle."

Once in the shade of the trees, I sit against the scratchy side of a pine and close my eyes for several breaths. The men drop their backpacks and layout.

"Zenner," Mazas says, snapping me back to reality. "We need to take inventory."

I blink against the dryness of my eyes and say, "Right."

Mazas and Brissanet spread blankets out, and Longchamps instructs everyone, "Go through your gear. Remove food and water."

The men lazily comply, rummaging through their packs, and then go back to resting. I remove my journal and sharpen my pencil with a folding knife. "Ready?" Mazas asks. I nod, testing the sharpness of the charcoal with my thumb, and he speaks out the count. We have among us to share, six cans of corned beef, thirteen cans of sardines, five kilograms of hard cheese, and two dozen loaves of stiff bread, each only a half meter long. For drinks, we have seven two-liter canteens, eleven one-liter canteens, and nine bottles of champagne. Of course, there are enough cigarettes to last forever.

"For the eighteen of us," Longchamps says, looking over my shoulder as I scribble the numbers, "we have one more full day's ration. Two, if we stretch it out." We look at one another, and he adds, "Three days' worth of food, they told us. Three days' worth. And to think of how much we left behind." He shakes his head.

Mazas starts repacking the food and handing back the canteens. "We'll pass Besancon soon enough, and there will be plenty of food to find after."

I light a cigarette and write in my journal as the men close their eyes. I want to record the town names I remember from the last few days. We might die on this journey, and someone will find my papers and know our struggle.

At some point, I must have closed my eyes because the next thing I knew, Voulard was nudging my shoulder. "Wake up," he says. "We have to go. Listen." He raises a finger, and I hear it. Faint explosions, along with the rattling of heavy artillery.

"Where is it coming from?" I ask, struggling to my feet.

Voulard shrugs, and Longchamps says, "Vesoul, I think."

"From this distance?" I shield my face from the sun, looking for planes. The far horizon in the direction of Vesoul is stained gray with smoke as if storm clouds had rolled toward us.

"It's possible," he says. "We've skirted along the city, but it's not far. Sounds like a ground assault. If we're lucky, the Germans are stalled there. Come on, let's go."

We walk single file with Longchamps in the lead, and I take up the rear. The day grows blistering hot as we travel the crest of hills, listening to the explosions echo. As the hours pass, the discord dulls and eventually stops altogether.

"It's strange," I hear Voulard say to Billet, "I think I'd rather hear the noise of warfare to at least know where the Germans are."

"You have a point," Billet says.

We walk, smoke cigarette after cigarette, and speak in short intervals. Our canteens are already running low, and I know from my growing hunger that we all must eat and will soon be out of food. It's a terrible thought.

"Wait." Longchamps raises a fist. We all stop. From the vantage, we see a farmhouse below. The roof is covered in moss, and vining plants have been woven into the brick framework. "Come on," he says and leads us down the embankment.

An elderly farmer emerges from the front door and stands with his hands in his pockets until we are near.

"Hello," Longchamps says, and the rest of us say hello or wave.

The farmer nods, his hands still in his pockets. "Don't have any food if that's what you're after."

"How about some water?" Longchamps taps the canteen strapped to his belt.

He turns toward his home, motioning us to follow.

We take turns filling our canteens from a spigot and give the man a few packs of cigarettes, which he happily takes. He asks about what we've seen and heard, and we tell him that Paris has fallen and that the Wehrmacht has attacked Vesoul and might still be attacking. It appears they are fast on our heels.

Mazas asks the man, "Do you have anywhere to go?"

"No," the man says. "I'll be okay. There's nothing for them to take if they come through here. A few cans of food—I'm sorry that I don't have enough to go around—but nothing more."

"We understand," Longchamps says, then bids the farmer farewell. The man stands next to his sagging home as we walk away. The vines seem to be holding it together more than tearing it apart.

As the day goes on, our exhaustion grows. Voulard and Piffet are last in line, and Mazas and I urge them forward. "We need rest," Voulard pleads.

"We will, soon enough," I tell him. "Just a little farther. You can make it." It's a lie because we continue for hours. Still, I tell him, "We'll stop soon." As evening approaches, Piffet and Voulard are on the verge of collapse. We ate most of our food earlier, leaving us with stale bread and some cheese. When we finish this meal, we will be out of rations.

"There's a town ahead." Longchamps points out. "Let's check for food."

As we enter, a sign reads *Providence*.

"It's deserted," Mazas says to no one in particular.

"It appears so," Longchamps answers. "Everyone, split up in twos. We'll meet in the plaza in half an hour. Keep your flashlight use minimal."

I go with Brissanet to the nearest home, and we knock before entering despite being relatively sure that no one is inside. The door is unlocked and opens to a cavernous interior. We go straight to the kitchen and inspect the cabinets, but there is nothing to take. Not a single grain of rice. We check four more homes to no avail. All are wiped clean. We meet back in the plaza, and Longchamps says, "We got two boxes of sugar cubes, almost empty, and three bottles of wine. We need to move on. If the town has been evacuated, it's for good reason."

A bottle of wine is opened and passed around. Mazas doles the sugar cubes, and I pop mine in my mouth, grinding the crystals between my teeth. The sugar has an effect on everyone, boosting our energy. Even Voulard and Piffet complain less.

We come to a road on the other side of town and walk along a stretch of abandoned vehicles. Some are nothing more than dark, burned, twisted shells, but others are in good condition. We go from one to the other, trying to start their engines, although most are out of petrol. Mazas finds a truck in good repair with fuel in its tank, but the engine won't turn over. "Come on," he says. "Come on … *start!*" Then, an engine rumbles to life from somewhere behind us, and we all turn to see a truck pull out from the line of vehicles. Longchamps is driving, and he shouts, "It won't stop; the brakes are barely working! Jump on!"

Everyone begins running at once. The truck is not going fast, so it's easy to catch. I climb aboard the flatbed and reach behind me to help Brissanet get on board. Piffet manages on his own, but Voulard needs help.

The truck continues slowly, with the rear tire deflated and shredding over the pavement. "There's barely any petrol," Longchamps says.

We get about five kilometers farther when the truck stops, and the engine sputters and turns off. "Damn it," Longchamps says. Nobody leaves the transport. It's apparent how much we need this vehicle to work. "Let's push it up that hill, just a little further."

We get out, and with us all pushing, the truck moves along. At the top of the hill, we get back on, and Longchamps lets gravity coast us to the bottom, where a stretch of abandoned vehicles line the side of the road. "Check for fuel," Longchamps instructs, and we all jump off.

"There must be some," I tell Voulard, who falters as he steps off the flatbed. Nobody wants to go on foot again. Our toes and heels are blistered and bloody, and our exhaustion is worsened by the ever-present, gnawing hunger.

I search from one vehicle to another when a voice shouts, "I found some!" It's Weber. He runs to us, holding a canister.

"Thank God," Longchamps says. "It's not much, but it's something."

Everyone gets back on board as the fuel is added, and Longchamps turns the ignition. It sputters to life, and we continue driving up and over another hill. We travel half a kilometer when he cuts the engine and says, "Look there!" There's a truck identical to ours. He gets out and inspects it. It won't start, and two tires are flat—but two are full, so he searches for a jack.

"Give me a hand," he tells us all. Mazas reaches him first, and they get an inflated tire off. Weber and I begin to remove the shredded one from our truck.

As we switch the tire, an engine is heard up the road, and everyone freezes. My initial reaction is to hide, but only one solitary vehicle travels toward us.

Once it nears, I see it's a French military truck, twice the size of our own. It stops, and the driver and passenger get out.

"Where are you going?" the driver asks. Both men are wearing coveralls, not uniforms.

"South of Besancon," Mazas replies. "What about you? Are you soldiers?"

The men shake their heads, and the passenger drops a cigarette to the ground and grinds it out with his heel. "We live in Quenoche. Don't go to Besancon. The bridge has been dynamited."

"By us or the Germans?" Longchamps asks.

"Don't know, but we haven't seen any Germans. There might be another way across, but I'm not sure. Head to Quenoche, it's on the way to Besancon. Someone there might know."

"The town hasn't been evacuated?"

"The people won't leave. Here, follow me." The two men motion for us to the rear of their truck. With a metallic groan, the hinged door lowers. We huddle together, looking inside.

"Is that what I think it is?" I ask.

"Fuel," the driver answers. Inside are well over a dozen large barrels. "We've been going up and down the highway, giving petrol to those in need. We stumbled on this just hours ago. It's not much, but it's all we can do to help."

Longchamps places his hand on the driver's shoulder. "It is much appreciated."

"Take what you need. We've only seen three other drivers, and I wouldn't be surprised if you're the last ones before we have to go into hiding."

Mazas and Longchamps hoist themselves on board, and two more follow. They push and pull a barrel to the edge and gently nudge it over as four men wait to receive it. The two civilians help.

"There's five hundred liters in here!" Brissanet says. We all thank the men and give them cigarettes.

"Safe travels," the driver says and returns to the truck.

We load the fuel and get on board. The vehicle sags with the weight but starts up and moves forward. The eighteen of us are too many for the small flatbed. Even with everyone as packed together as can be, four have to hold on to the side, and I volunteer to be one of them. With the new tire, the drive is much smoother, and I feel a degree of hope for the first time. Knowing that Besancon is close and that once over, we will find food and arrive at a plan on where to go. That is, of course, dependent on just how quick the Wehrmacht travels and whether or not they pause before Besancon. I don't want to admit it, but I doubt they will halt anywhere long before taking over every stretch of French soil.

Chapter Nine
Quenoche

A road sign proceeds Quenoche, and people sit on the porch of the first building we pass. Large red letters painted on the side of the wall read, *Hotel, Café*. Longchamps halts and cuts the engine. The truck springs up with a creak as we disembark. A man sitting on the porch stands upon our arrival and waves.

Mazas waves back and asks, "Do you work here? Any chance you have food for sale?"

The man adjusts his cap. "I'm sorry, but we don't. Our kitchen ran dry, and there's no way to get to Besancon to restock. We have some beer, though." He motions us into the café.

The men file in, and I stay with Mazas to talk to the civilians on the porch. The man tells us he's the establishment's proprietor, and the other two, an elderly couple seated sipping from thick beer steins, remain silent. Mazas shake their hands in turn, and I do the same. Longchamps joins us, holding three mugs. He passes me one, and I ask the proprietor, "So it's true, the bridge to Besancon has been demolished?"

The man nods. "Unfortunately."

"Is there another way to cross the Doubs?"

"None so close to Besancon that I've discovered. We've heard that Paris has fallen. Do you know this to be true?"

"It is."

The elderly man shakes his head, his face in a scowl. "We let the bastards walk right in." His voice is a hoarse croak. His wife retorts, "Language!" The old man waves at her dismissively and sips his beer.

"This is the first town we've come across that isn't evacuated," Mazas says. "You should leave."

They seem to think it over, and then the proprietor asks, "Have you seen the Germans? Are they close?"

"Last we saw, Vesoul was being bombed," I tell him. "I'm afraid to say that Dijon is under their control, and I would venture to guess the same in Nancy and Sarrebourg."

The three of them are quiet, casting their gazes to the ground. The north and west are under Nazi control, and the road to Besancon goes right through their little village.

"Do you know if there is any food in town?" Longchamps asks.

"The market was wiped out last I checked," he answers and hooks his thumbs in his suspenders. "But I don't know for sure."

I finish my glass and feel the alcohol absorb into my bloodstream, with little food to delay inebriation. The slight buzz is a nice escape, but I turn down a second glass, and we thank the man. Longchamps addresses the company assembled in the yard before the café. "Let's check in town and be quick about it."

We leave the truck and walk down a road with homes on either side among pastures. People emerge from doorways, watching as we near the village center. By their gazes, I guess that few uniformed soldiers have passed through this small town, and the sight of us is causing a hushed gossip. The church's steeple rises above the rooftops, the cross in full view to bless wandering eyes. The gentle sound of a running stream grows pronounced as we near. A man in priestly attire steps out from a tall wooden door with stained glass adorned above and motions for us to come inside. "Please," he says. "Come in and pray, and accept my prayers for you, soldiers."

Some of our company step forward, and Longchamps says, "Five minutes." They nod their agreeance.

Growing up, I was never forced to attend church, primarily due to its distance from the farm and that my time was needed in the fields. However, I was made to fear the implications of turning my back on religion. I'm starting to see otherwise, that all the prayer in the world won't stop evils such as the Nazi party from poisoning the soil they trample. It's hard to fathom that any God would allow murder and hatred to blossom so freely and on such a scale. Watching the men disappear into the shadowy church, I'm suspicious that their praying will be in vain and the time better spent searching for supplies.

The rest of us speak to the townspeople on the streets, standing at doorways until we find the market. A group of farmers have assembled, drinking wine. They call us over and offer open bottles. "Thank you," Longchamps says and accepts the handout. He isn't given a glass, so he drinks from the bottle and passes it to me. "Is there any food?"

A heavy-set older man shakes his head. "I'm afraid not." His teeth and lips are stained red. "I'm the owner." He reaches out and shakes Longchamps' hand. "Please, stay and drink."

"We must continue on, and I suggest you do the same. Does anyone know where we can find a bridge over the Doubs?"

"Yes," another man chimes in. "There's a town south of here and east of Besancon. Are you going on foot? It's over thirty kilometers."

"We have a truck."

The young man's face lights up. "Do you have room for one more? I need to make it to Grenoble, farther to the south, but I will gladly take a ride as far as you can venture. I will lead you to the bridge. I know the roads."

Longchamps accepts the man's proposal but says, "You'll have to hold on to the side of the truck. We don't all fit as it is. One of the tires has formed a bulge from the weight, and I'm afraid it will pop at any given moment."

"What kind of truck is it?" another man asks before sipping his glass.

"A Citroen," Longchamps says and gives the details.

The man places his glass tumbler on a weathered crate used as a table and wipes a sleeve over his mouth. "Wait here. I will only be a minute." With that, he stands and walks away.

In his absence, I tell the group, "You should leave, go south. The Germans were right behind us in Vesoul and don't appear to be slowing."

The men sip their wine in contemplation, and the market proprietor says, "Some have left, but you must understand that this is our home. There are no soldiers here, no defenses. We hold no significance to the Germans."

I nod. "All the same, if you have somewhere you can go, you should leave."

"Where would be safer than where we are? The Germans will pass right through."

"Perhaps."

A few minutes later, the man who left reappears, holding a small wooden box. "Here," he says. "Take it." He holds the box out for Longchamps to open. Inside is an inner tube. "I have no use for it."

Longchamps thanks the man and asks, "Are you sure you won't need it? Do you farm?"

The man shakes his head. "I'm a teacher."

We thank the gathering, and Mazas tells me, "It's inspiring to see such selflessness."

The man heading to Grenoble introduces himself as Raymond, and he joins us in collecting our company from the church. We board our small truck and turn our sights back on the road.

***

It is ten at night and very dark. The barren villages are shadowy, with the outlines of buildings guiding us. There is light ahead, a beacon in the distance. As we approach, two soldiers appear standing at a fork in the road like apparitions. Several candles are burning on a table beside them, the little dancing flames cutting through the darkness like blades.

They are aroused at our approach and motion for us to stop. Longchamps cuts the engine, but we all stay onboard. "Where are you going?" one of the soldiers asks.

"Baume-les-Dames," Longchamps answers. "We've heard there is a bridge intact."

The soldier nods. "Turn right." He motions us onward, and we continue. We don't drive for long until we see the taillights of a vehicle ahead and catch up to the rear of an ambulance. We follow it toward the town and pass a stalled truck full of people with the hood open and then an army truck with three soldiers smoking cigarettes beside it. The congestion of vehicles increases, and we halt in a long procession, taillights reflecting a sea of red against the pavement. There are more ambulances, farmers with caged animals and packed suitcases, several tanks, troop transports, and all manner of civilian and army vehicles. The line stretches indefinitely, and many automobiles have turned off their engines.

"I'll scout ahead," I offer.

Mazas and Weber join me, and we walk in the line, asking the occasional person if they know why there is so much traffic. They all shrug, and a few ask for cigarettes. We walk for almost half an hour until we come to the end of the line, where a dozen Foreign Legion soldiers guard the bridge, distinguished by their round caps and tan uniforms.

They acknowledge us, and I ask a soldier, "Why is the bridge closed?"

"We don't know."

"But you're keeping it shut?"

"We've been ordered to keep the bridge closed until sunrise."

"And you don't know why?"

"No."

The man rests his hand on his rifle strap and offers nothing more. We return to the line of vehicles and tell the groups of people standing beside their automobiles what the Foreign Legion soldiers told us.

Back at our truck, Longchamps leans out the driver's side window, smoking a cigarette. "Well?" He flicks an ash into the darkness.

"The bridge is closed until morning," I tell him and explain.

"Nonsense," he says, "But we might as well get some rest."

Some men have already deboarded and are sitting on the grass beside the road or mingling with other soldiers and civilians. Upon hearing that we aren't moving until morning, everyone finds blankets to lay out on. I sit on the grass and write for a duration in my journal, using the glow of headlights and the reflection of taillights to see the pages cast in a varying hue. It is now after midnight, and exhaustion is fast approaching. I lay out and close my eyes, thinking anxiety will keep me awake, yet my fatigue is more significant. Then, all at once—I'm snapped out of a heavy slumber. The convoy rumbles to life as hundreds of engines turn on at once. It must be morning, but the sky is still dark. My brain is deep in unconsciousness when I hear, "Zenner! Come on!"

I jump to my feet, blanket in one hand, journal in the other, and run to the back of the truck as it moves. My head is swimming, and I look at the time, confused that it is still pitch-black. It's two in the morning, and we are moving toward the bridge. It isn't long until I see the Foreign Legion on the side of the road, motioning the procession over the river and shouting, "Keep your headlights off!"

My eyes are swollen, and I try to rub them awake as I ask Longchamps, "They didn't wait until morning?"

He shrugs.

On either side, the River Doubs glimmers moonlight as we cross the bridge—the first that doesn't blow up on us. I sigh with relief as we make it to the other side. We will find safety after Besancon, where the Wehrmacht will get held up. But of course, to make it to Besancon, we must navigate a treacherous mountain pass in the dead of night without headlights to aid us.

Chapter Ten
Difficulty in the Night

The gridlock creeps forward in a single-file line. On the right, the mountains loom. To the left, the moon reflects a million silver blades along the dark river below. Voulard and I walk in front of our truck, keeping our backs against the ambulance's bumper preceding us. We each hold a white handkerchief high overhead so Longchamps knows when to slow or stop and avoid the rocky edge. He yells out the window, "Raise it higher!" There is no guardrail to halt a sudden plummet. Voulard and I chain-smoke cigarettes, using the glowing tips to help guide Longchamps. An accident high up here would be terrible, and I think of the tanks and transports driving ahead. I can't help but imagine them breaking down, running out of fuel, popping a tire, and engines overheating. How would we pass? Hundreds of vehicles would be stuck, and everyone would have to navigate on foot in the dark.

"Hey," Voulard says. "Look there. What is that?" I turn to see a white cloth tied to a stake in the ground, and I peer ahead around the ambulance.

"Someone marked the side of the road," I say with relief. "It continues." The white material, a paper of sorts, stretches on. It doesn't help Longchamps, but I know where the road ends and the cliff begins.

We come to sudden and frequent stops, and during one of them, Ross takes the wheel, and Longchamps sits in the passenger seat. Ross is better rested, yet still, he calls out to Voulard and myself, "I can barely see!"

The truck veers to the left, and I jump while waving my arms. "Stop, Ross! Stop!"

The truck halts with the front tire skirting the sharp boundary. Sweat drips down my cheeks, and I yell to him, "Cut the wheel!" As the truck creeps forward, shifting, I hear pebbles fall from the cut-off and roll down the cliff. With everyone piled on top, the truck's weight could have toppled our little Citroen head over heels if he drove a few centimeters further. Nightmare fantasies play out in my thoughts of my friends attempting to jump out as the vehicle flips, crushing those on the sides and in the flatbed before continuing to tumble down like a child's toy. Would anyone from the convoy try to help us? Would anyone even be able to see the wreckage?

I wipe sweat from my eyes, grab a yard or so of the white paper that had been ripped and trampled, and hand Voulard a portion. We hold them aloft like flags, warning Ross of the perils. "Straight!" I shout. "Keep going straight!"

Another hour passes, and we no longer see the river, and the mountain wall on our other side flattens out. It is five a.m., and the sky is cracking to a pale dawn.

"If only we had a fraction of this light during the night," I say to Voulard. My eyes feel sunken in their sockets, the skin around them puffy and raw.

Voulard and I climb aboard, and I'm happy Longchamps is sleeping. Instead of hanging onto the side, I sit on the roof and scribble in my journal as the traffic crawls onward. The panorama is inspiring; rolling green hills with sporadic climbing pines and oaks. It's a relief that we made it through the night. It's cold at this high altitude, especially with my shirt wet from perspiring from sheer stress, so I wrap myself in a blanket as we descend the other side of the mountain pass.

I am the first to spot it and shout, "Look up ahead!"

An inn sits on the side of the road, with dozens of vehicles parked in front and twice that number of bicycles. Several horse-drawn carts are among them, and I can't help but feel that horse carriages are a better way to travel. The animals sense the ground better and navigate most obstacles better than we do.

The engine is cut, and we all go in, except for Ross, who stays to guard the truck. Warmth engulfs me as we step inside, and people are so closely crammed in that it takes several minutes until we reach the head of the line. The weary face of an old shopkeeper stares at us from across the counter, and I ask him, "Do you have any food? Hot coffee?"

He shakes his head. "We have milk. That's it. We've run out of everything."

It's unsurprising, given that his establishment has more customers now than he sees in a season.

"Milk, then," I order. "Warm, if possible."

He nods, calls the order to someone in the back, and then turns to us. "That will be fourteen twenty-five."

I'm appalled, and Mazas says, "Wait a minute, that's ... seventy-five cents a cup?"

The man nods unapologetically.

"There are more cows than people in these mountains," Mazas says.

"Be sure to bring the cups back," the man says, ignoring Mazas's response. I feel the press of people behind our group, and we gather our money and pay.

"What a rip-off," Mazas grumbles as we walk back outside. The men follow, cupping their warm milk in their palms. Ross is in the driver's seat with blankets over him. "Here." Mazas hands him a warm cup. Ross blows back the steam and takes a sip. He sighs and closes his eyes, wrapping his hands around the mug. "It cost seventy-five cents a cup," Mazas says.

"Let it go," Longchamps cuts in. "What's more important, money or warm milk in your stomach?"

Mazas looks into his cup and shrugs, but he stops complaining. He glances at the farmland, where the ringing of cowbells is incessant, and shakes his head.

Longchamps has a map out over the truck's hood, and we gather around as his finger trails the page. "We're twenty kilometers from Pontarlier," he says. I know of Pontarlier but have never been there. It's a large city that produces anise, which is sold throughout France and beyond. In its early days, Pontarlier produced absinthe. I remember my stepfather having a bottle back when I was a little boy and him explaining how the liquor is supposed to be dripped over a sugar cube. However, he drank it with a bit of water. "Normally, it would take us under a half hour to get there," Longchamps continues. "But given our situation ... it's hard to say."

"Pontarlier?" a voice says from outside our group. We see a man holding the reins atop a horse carriage. "Is that what you said?"

"That's right," Longchamps responds.

"You'd be best to avoid it. The Germans will be there by noon, latest."

"How do you know this?" I ask.

"Talk to any of the soldiers. I'm surprised you haven't heard," he says, pointing to our uniforms.

We look at one another, and I check my watch. It's eight in the morning.

"Let's go," Longchamps says and folds the map. "We need to get in and past Pontarlier before the Germans."

Chapter Eleven
Tuesday, 18 June, 1940

We park on the outskirts of Pontarlier and make trips inside the town center to try to find food. One restaurant has coffee, and we pack in with soldiers from various companies and nationalities. Some wear Belgian uniforms, and we spot two from England. They all drink and leave, knowing the Germans are fast approaching.

Voulard is first in line and orders for us all. They have some cookies left, twelve in total—what luck! He buys them all, and we take our coffee to the back of the restaurant to divide up the cookies. None of the soldiers we see wear weapons. They are all from non-fighting units, like our own.

An older man nearby asks, "Where are you coming from?"

"Sarrebourg," I tell him.

"And where are you going?"

After a pause, I say, "South."

The man nods. "My nephew has farmland in Vaux-et-Chantegrue." He sips his coffee, sighs, then continues, "First opportunity I get, I'll change out of this blasted uniform. Every store is out of goods, clothing, food, everything. I'll ask residents for a pair of pants and a shirt. If the Germans catch up—when they catch up—I'll tell them I'm a farmer."

"Do you think you'll be safe at your nephew's farm? They've shown little sympathy to civilians. In Poland, I heard hundreds were executed each day. More civilians than military. I can't imagine what they're doing to our people in the north."

"Yes, I've heard the same about Poland. But it's the best I can come up with. Staying in France is a gamble; I would try to get to the Swiss border, but I would be leaving my family behind. At least in Vaux-et-Chantegrue, my home in Orleans is one day of travel. I pray that the Germans will better regard the French than the Polish, but that is yet to be seen." The man finishes his coffee and wipes his beard with a sleeve. "Good luck to you," he says, bringing his cup and saucer to the counter. I hope the man is correct in saying that the German army is more considerate toward the French, but I have doubts.

I return to the group just as Longchamps says, "We need to get moving." We finish our coffee and file out. Nothing is open. The stores are wiped clean, yet some people remain as if it were an ordinary day. Denial, perhaps. Or maybe they have nowhere to go or feel they wouldn't be safer somewhere else. We pass a church, and I marvel at the black tile roof and ornate clock embedded high on the wall. The gold embellishment glistens, and the adornment in the center is the same shade of blue as a clear sky. The door opens and shuts, with a stream of civilian and military personnel making the sign of the cross as they enter and exit. Church walls can't shield bullets, yet I keep my thoughts to myself.

Our truck is parked half a kilometer away, and when we get there, Mazas wakes Brissanet, who'd been left to watch over our possessions. Brissanet opens his eyes with a start but is thankful for the cup of coffee Mazas hands him.

"It's cold," Brissanet says. "But it's great." He drains it back as we pile in the truck and grab hold of the sides. The engine rumbles to life.

For the first time, traffic is moving. We're going fifty kilometers an hour as we exit Pontarlier. Still, the going isn't easy with all the vehicles trying to pass one another, and an unending line of broken-down automobiles stretch on either side of the road. More than once, I see a person hit by a bicyclist while trying to fix their engine or tire. On one occasion, a soldier is sleeping in the grass beside a truck being repaired, and a cyclist runs right over his legs without stopping. The man wakes in a jolt and curses, but the rider is long gone.

Others are on horseback or horse-drawn carriages, and I again feel this is the best way to travel. Not once have I seen a dead horse on the side of the road. But vehicles? Hundreds, perhaps thousands. Many people go on foot, walking and running on the field bordering the road. Soldiers mostly, but there are women, men, children, and the elderly. Their faces are grave, panicked. If we had room, we would take as many as possible.

Pontarlier vanishes as we travel, and soon we are a kilometer away, and then two.

"We might just outrun the Germans yet!" Brissanet shouts. "Look ahead—vehicles are moving as far as the eye can see!"

I smile, sharing in his hope, yet unable to shake the knowledge of how close the Wehrmacht is at our heels. They will be in Pontarlier soon; without the city's defenses, they will walk right in. Where they go from there is unknown. I guess they will continue to spread at record speed, to poison every patch of countryside.

"To think," Brissanet continues as he pulls a cigarette from the pack with his teeth. "Last month, the Nazis were still in Germany. Two weeks ago, there was hope they could be pushed back despite the disaster at Dunkirk. And now, here they are, over five hundred kilometers from the Maginot Line, which should have halted them."

"It's a disgrace—"

The truck jolts.

"Shit!" Ross shouts from the driver's seat. Horns blare around us. He straightens out, but the truck drives as if on rough terrain.

My heart sinks, knowing before Longchamps shouts, "The tire blew!"

Ross navigates to the side of the road, among the cemetery of vehicles, and turns off the engine. We spill out and stare at the shredded fibers attached to the exposed rim.

"God damn it!" Mazas' hands are in fists. "We can't be more than three fucking kilometers away from Pontarlier and actually moving for the first fucking time!" He punches the side of the truck. "Damn it!"

The sentiment carries over the men, yet Longchamps remains calm. "See if there's another stalled truck nearby with the same size tire." He searches the flatbed for the toolbox and takes it to the ground. Inside is the inner tube from the schoolteacher in Quenoche. Longchamps shakes his head. "The wall is too shredded to change the inner tube only. We need a whole tire."

"We don't have time to change an inner tube anyway," Mazas says, making a clicking noise in his mouth. "We barely have time to change the tire." He looks at his wrist, still without a watch, and Longchamps tells him it's twelve thirty-five.

Everyone searches the abandoned vehicles when five minutes later, Longchamps calls us back together. "We have to leave the truck," he says. "We're too close to Pontarlier to stay any longer."

I'm disheartened. The vehicle has been so helpful. But Longchamps is right—we can't wait. Voulard, Billet, and Batist start unloading our gear to the side of the road. Stationed at a junction ahead are about twenty armed soldiers and a captain looking in bewilderment over the sea of traffic. They have several machine-gun posts and one sizeable anti-tank gun. Longchamps and Mazas go to speak to them. The soldiers' faces show their exhaustion, much like our own. I wait while the gear is being unloaded, trying to put some order in the pile of belongings.

People walking across the field beside us begin to run, a few at first, but then more. "Go!" one of them shouts. "Run! The Germans are in Pontarlier!" The news is spread by panicked voices, and we start grabbing our bags. A soldier passes and shouts, "They've crossed!" Longchamps and Mazas hurry back, and we take off fast, leaving the truck and the crates of supplies. We run with the herd of soldiers, bicycles, and clomping horses for about a kilometer, then Longchamps directs us off the road and into the woods. Others follow, yet the majority stick to the road.

The ground is rocky here, and some stumble and are helped back up. There is no path, but we can see the River Doubs on our side through the thicket of trees and use it as a guide. We go faster than we should, and I feel a sting on my cheek and the pull of a thorned vine as it grabs my skin. When I touch my face, there is blood on my fingers.

But I don't stop for a second and stay beside Voulard, who has tripped and stumbled more than once. I hold on to his arm near the elbow and guide him. "Come on, Voulard. Mind where you're going!"

We pass a low barbed wire fence, and beyond the trees is pasture. The ground is soft and springy, and the mud is thick. Other than our panting, the only sound comes from cowbells. The trees return on the other side of the pasture, and the ground elevates to a rocky incline. Voulard is wheezing, grabbing the sides of trees to pull himself onward, and I help push him along. The hill is not large, but the backpacks make the climb difficult, and when we reach the top, we stop. I double over, taking large inhalations.

We are startled to see others already there, hiding on the hilltop. Mothers with babies, kids, men, and elderly. They must be from the neighboring town of Oye-et-Pallet, and a few roofs of that same village are visible from our vantage point. The road leading into the city is lined with abandoned automobiles. A few dozen French soldiers are stationed on either side, manning machine-gun nests, attempting to keep order as they await the crush of the German army from the north.

Chapter Twelve
Gunfire and Cowbells

We ask the townspeople hiding in the woods if they know how close the Germans are, but they don't. Brissanet speaks to an older gentleman who is sitting atop his suitcase. "Our soldiers stationed at the entrance to town worries me. How will thirty men stop the force of the Wehrmacht?" The man opens his palms in a futile gesture. "They won't. Some of us tried to reason with them and told those young men to leave while they could, but their commanding officer was adamant they hold their position. All they will achieve is to further enrage the Germans, and the citizens stuck in the middle will be punished."

I turn my attention to Longchamps, who is talking to a young couple. The woman says, "I hope they march straight through … I want to go home." Her husband wipes sweat from his forehead with a handkerchief and adds, "We shouldn't be waiting here to find out. We need to leave, all of us. We can return after the fighting."

All the citizens tell a similar tale. One of fear and apprehension. I don't blame them. The men in our company try to calm their worry, and some even want to go to the village to sleep. Weber says, "We have time. There's no reason for the Germans to hurry south to Oye-et-Pallet. There's no strategic value here."

Voulard nods his agreeance, and Ross says, "He's right. We could find a home on the outskirts and take turns keeping vigil. When the Germans approach, we'll have time to return to the woods."

Most of the others in our company do not agree. Staying in the woods is far safer. Longchamps says, "If we had our truck, we'd be far from here by now."

There's a cold wind filtering through the trees, and the men drape blankets over their shoulders. I go to my backpack to do the same and discover my blanket is missing. "It can't be …" I rummage through the backpack again, but it's pointless. "It's in the truck. It has to be. Damn it!"

Longchamps stands beside me. "Let's ask the soldiers in town if they have a spare blanket, just the two of us. Better yet, maybe they'll know of a working truck somewhere or at least a tire for ours. We might have time to make the repair before the Wehrmacht reaches the road."

I look over my shoulder in the direction of Oye-et-Pallet. There's no indication that the Germans are close; no loud engines, bullet fire, or explosions.

"All right," I agree. "Let's go."

We stand and start walking, and Brissanet runs to catch up. "I'm coming. If they have a tire, it will be quicker to repair with three of us."

As the hill declines, the ground clears to grassy pasture, and we walk past homes to enter the small plaza at the town's entrance. A few residents still walk about looking indifferent, as if the soldiers stationed nearby and the long line of fleeing vehicles are an everyday occurrence.

"Hey," Brissanet says and stops to point. "Hold up." There's a small fountain skirting the side of the plaza, more of a stone watering hole for horses. We walk over and take turns drinking the ice-cold water, taking scoops in our palms. I splash the water over my face and feel a surge of life return to my veins.

"We'll have the men come down and fill their canteens," Longchamps says.

I use a handkerchief to wipe water from my face as we wave to the soldiers stationed at a small artillery piece set on rails. Two machine-gun posts parallel the cannon, one on either side of the road, behind sandbag walls. A few turn and wave back as we approach, and an older man with a gray beard motions us over. "Hello!" he calls out. We shake his hand in turn. He wears sergeant insignia on the sleeve of his uniform, and as we shake, he says, "Sergeant Bonfils. Where are you boys coming from?"

We introduce ourselves, and Longchamps tells him a rushed tale. The man nods as he listens and stuffs tobacco into a pipe with his thumb. Nothing he hears is surprising. When Longchamps tells him of the missing blanket, the old man says, "We have plenty in the warehouse. No rations, though." He stops to strike a match and brings the pipe to flame, then continues through puffs, "The Germans have occupied Pontarlier, and we expect them on the road ahead."

"How long?" Brissanet asks.

"We will hear the guns at Fort de Joux fire on them as they near, and I expect the Wehrmacht will be held up before arriving at our position. There's been no commotion from the fort or reports that the Germans are advancing, so I suspect we have some time. Come, I'll take you to the warehouse." He motions for us to follow as he turns, adjusting the rifle strap on his shoulder.

"Where's Fort de Joux?" Brissanet asks.

"Seven kilometers north. You must have taken to the woods before passing it, otherwise you would have seen the stone fortification high in the mountains. It can't be missed. The building is hundreds of years old but was updated with armored walls, cannons, and machine-gun nests. It guards the road to Pontarlier and the pass from Switzerland should the Germans invade from the east. The Wehrmacht won't have an easy time passing. Our boys will give 'em a bit of sport yet."

I've heard of the Fort de Joux from passing soldiers when we were stationed in Sarrebourg. The structure is high up on the point of a mountain and is considered to be part of the Maginot Line.

The sergeant leads us away from the front line and down narrow lanes. The town comprises of thin rows of homes and buildings along either side of the few streets and nothing more. Behind the buildings are never-ending stretches of farmland. The sergeant's sweet-smelling tobacco smoke trails behind as we follow, and then he turns to a home.

"Here we are," he says and shows us inside. A lone soldier stands as we enter and nods to the officer. "It's a shame," the sergeant motions to the many crates of munitions pilled in the front room, "the shells are for large caliber. Useless, all of it." We follow him down a narrow hallway, with boxes stacked to the ceiling along one wall and to a bedroom in the back. "Here," he says and enters the room. He moves a few boxes and finds one with blankets folded neatly inside. "This should do."

I thank the man and accept the blanket.

"Do you need any ammunition? We have plenty of Mas thirty-six rounds and even two crates of Mas thirty-eight. Are you even armed?" He looks us up and down.

"No," Longchamps says.

We follow the sergeant back outside, leaving the lone guard to sit back down. Then we hear the distant clatter of gunfire, unceasing. "That's the fort." The sergeant turns to us with a smile. "Who knows, maybe we'll halt their advance yet!"

We smile back, but after the Germans took Dijon and Pontarlier in record time, I doubt a single fort high in the mountains will offer much help. However, I'm optimistic that the Wehrmacht will be stalled.

Back at the machine-gun nest, I again thank the officer, and he calls for one of his men to give a report on the German advance. We're delighted to hear that they are held up. "We have maps of the local area," the sergeant tells us. "Do you need one?"

"Yes," Longchamps says. "Thank you."

The sergeant calls for another soldier and takes a map from him. He lays it out beside the field artillery on a table and trails a finger across the page.

"There's Switzerland," Brissanet says. "It's only, what ... thirteen kilometers from here?"

"About," I say. "But there are no direct roads in or out."

"I suggest you head further south," the sergeant says. "The Germans will have these eastern routes closed off before the day is done. Head toward Gex. It's a journey on foot but a safer path to the Swiss border."

Longchamps folds the map. "We can't thank you enough." He shakes the sergeant's hand.

"Any chance I can convince you boys to stay and help our unit? We have spare rifles."

We are quiet for a moment, and perhaps we should. We have little hope of outrunning the German war machine, no matter which direction we go.

Brissanet's eyes widen. He has a family, a wife and children. I've seen him stare at their pictures for hours at a time. He keeps them in an inner pocket near his heart.

Longchamps makes the final decision. "We've come a long way. We will continue onward. The Swiss border is our best option."

"Good luck." The sergeant gives us a nod.

Again, we thank the kind man and head back to the company and the civilians in the woods. Brissanet asks me as we walk, "You want to stay and fight, don't you?"

"To be honest," I tell him. "I don't know."

He looks to his feet and says, "You have a girlfriend back home? Or a job waiting?"

I'm not sure why he asks. I never once spoke of having a girlfriend in all this time together. I've talked at length about moving to Paris a few years before the war, and the women who live there; beautiful and plentiful, unlike anything imaginable after growing up on a farm. I've spoken about my desire to marry, have a family. I've shared the most intimate of details about my inspirations and desires. He knows about my street performances, doing flips and balancing acts for a coin or two from passersby. I've garnered a few girlfriends, inspired by my standing upside down on one hand, or atop the shoulders of my co-performer. But nothing that lasted longer than a few dates. By now, he would know if I had a girl waiting for me. He also knows that my acrobatic troupe was gaining popularity before the war and that there were hopes of us performing at the cabarets and circuses. But before I left Paris, nothing was scheduled.

"No," I say. "No girlfriend. I have a profession, though, in a bakery." He knows this as well.

"One day, you'll have a wife. Children, maybe. You'll understand. This war … I can't fathom how a German soldier who has something, someone to lose back home, can go about this terrible business."

I nod.

"What I'm saying," he continues, "it's not just about fearing death. Everyone fears it, even the most valiant. Taking somebody else's life is a whole other matter. If I can go my years without removing a father, husband, or son from this earth, I will. If I thought that making a stand would make the slightest difference, protect my home and family, I would gladly take up arms. But that small group of soldiers, they are all going to die. They will make widows of their wives, and their children will grow up without fathers. This war …" He shakes his head. "It is about survival right now. It's about making it through the German invasion alive so that we can regather after the dust settles and come up with a logical plan to get them off our soil. Nothing will come from a few soldiers making a foolish stand."

I don't answer. I disagree, but it's better to not air my differences. We are together, what is left of our unit, and as Lieutenant Serre told me at the beginning of this trek, I must do everything in my power to help Longchamps lead the others to safety.

When we enter the woods, Mazas stands at the head of the group. "Well?" he asks. "That's bullet fire; you hear it?" We tell him what we learned: that the Germans are held up momentarily. Longchamps unfolds the map he'd been given.

The gunfire goes on for hours, and we try to rest, but it's impossible. Although far off, the clamor puts everyone on edge. Then, just as suddenly as it began, the discord stops. There are a few pops and rattles, but nothing more than that.

"That's it," Longchamps says. "The Germans have taken the fort."

I look at him, unable to hide my grim demeanor. A few of the civilians cry, and that is the only noise besides the cowbells. Longchamps tells us to move further into the thicket, and we oblige. Yet, a handful of citizens remain, believing their cover sufficient. We find a small clearing and sit with our backs against trees. The gunfire returns louder, and we know the Germans have reached Oye-et-Pallett. Soon after, screams pierce the woods.

Chapter Thirteen
Oye-et-Pallet

Piffet shakes with each succession of bullet fire and says in a whisper, "Jesus, they're c-close." Everyone is low to the ground, elderly and children alike. Mothers are hushing their babies, showering their little faces in hot tears. Ross and Batist scouted the opposite side of the woods after the gunfire ceased at Fort de Joux and saw a procession of German-armed vehicles and tanks along a minor road. We are surrounded to the north, east, and west. The sergeant in Oye-et-Pallet was right; we can't walk a direct path as close as we are to the Swiss border.

There is movement in the woods, and a man stumbles in the thicket, clutching his stomach. He leans against a tree for support and then takes wobbly steps toward us. Nobody goes to his aid. We sink closer to the earth, and I scan the thicket behind him for movement. Finally, Brissanet runs to the man, staying low, and then Mazas follows. They grab him by his biceps and bring him to where we are gathered, stealing glances over their shoulders.

"Th-they sh-shot into the w-woods," the man says. A rivulet of deep red trickles between his clutched fingers. He's not a soldier.

Longchamps and I join Mazas, Brissanet, and three civilians at the man's side, pressing handkerchiefs against the flowing blood, and one of the civilians removes his jacket. The injured man groans, and we tell him to be quiet, please, try to be quiet. Longchamps finds his medical kit in his backpack and rips open bandage wrappers with his teeth. The gauze saturates at once.

"Were you followed?" Longchamps asks.

The man's eyes loll under their lids, and his skin is pale. "I d-don't know.

Th-the Germans s-stormed into t-town. One saw us, c-crouching in the w-woods."

"Did anyone else survive?"

"I-I don't know."

The gunfire slows to a few lone shots. Longchamps leaves the injured man to the civilians' care and splashes water from his canteen over his bloody hands. "We have to go," he says. We all nod our approval. After studying the map earlier, we found the best route is to skirt the town in a straight southern direction and stay in the woods.

"Hey," Mazas interjects, pointing into the thicket. "More are coming."

My heart pounds. Four uniformed men run toward us, clutching rifles and looking over their shoulders. One stumbles to his knees and rights himself back up. They are French soldiers, eyes large, hands noticeably trembling, uniforms disheveled.

"Are you injured?" Longchamps asks.

The men tremble, and two double over, out of breath. The tallest in the group has blood speckled over his face yet does not appear injured. "There must be a hundred Germans, maybe more," he says. "We held them up for a few minutes but were surrounded."

"Were you followed?"

The men look over their shoulders, and one says, "I don't think so."

"Did anyone else survive?"

They don't answer. Then the tall man says, "I don't know. The German's MGs had us pinned while they flanked our side." He shook his head and cast his eyes to the ground. "Half of us were ripped to shreds in the first minute. We were ordered to fall back into town, but there was a clear path to the woods, so we ran to the trees. It's over. The Germans have Oye-et-Pallet. Someone was screaming for a medic as we retreated, but there are no medics, no Red Cross."

Mazas hands the men a pack of cigarettes each and turns to Longchamps. "Ready?"

He nods. We tell the group that we're moving out and that they can join. I'm surprised that they all want to remain where they are. Fear has them stuck, hidden, if at least for a while. We turn and leave.

Truck engines are audible from the road as we skirt Oye-et-Pallet, and an occasional bullet shot rings out. A faint hint of woodsmoke permeates the clean mountain air. Piffet whispers, "You think there are any of the soldiers left in Oye-et-Pallet still fighting?"

I shake my head. "The Germans are most likely executing survivors. Maybe even citizens." We're silent for a moment, and then I add, "They're swine, the Germans, all of them."

It isn't long until the rumbling engines grow quieter and then cease entirely as we distance ourselves from roads and homes. There is a trace of water left in my canteen, and I hold it upside down over my mouth, letting the trickle fall to my tongue and absorb. None of us returned to the fountain to fill our canteens, and I debate asking Longchamps for a sip of his water.

We enter full pastureland with a magnificent panorama on all sides of rolling green hills under a crisp, clear sky. It's a strange paradox to notice beautiful things, yet we all do. Even Piffet—at the tail end of our procession along with Voulard—says, "I've never seen such gorgeous land." An hour ago, he had been trembling at the clamor of gunfire.

Others hold their canteens upside down over their open mouths, shaking droplets onto their tongues. Longchamps orders us to take a break under a scattering of pine trees, and I sit down with my back against the rough bark. "Who has water?" he asks. No one responds. Longchamps shakes his canteen and unscrews the cap. He takes a sip and wipes his mouth with a sleeve. "There's less than half a cup. I know you're all thirsty." He hands the canteen to Piffet. "One sip. That's all. Pass it on. We won't all get some."

Piffet puts his lips to the rim and closes his eyes as he takes a drink. He looks pained taking it away, but hands it to Voulard. I won't get any. But if I were Longchamps, I would have done the same. Despite the terrible dryness in my throat and the cramping in my stomach, Piffet and Voulard need water more than I need it.

My eyes close involuntarily, sleep wanting to pull me away. Longchamps is going from one man to the next, speaking softly, asking about blisters, headaches, and hunger. His voice pulls me from the edge of fantasy. "I'm worried about them," he whispers. I open my eyes and follow his gaze to Piffet and Voulard. My legs are throbbing from the exertion, and open wounds on my heels sting.

"Yes." My voice is hoarse. "I am, too."

"Stay with them in the rear. You and Mazas."

I nod, too weary to speak. Longchamps takes a study of me and asks, "Are you okay?"

Again, I nod.

"All right." He pats my shoulder. "We head out in five minutes. Rest." He points to tall hills over a large body of water in the valley below. "The Swiss border is over those mountains." With that, he turns and goes to the next man. My eyes close. The magical realm of sleep is so close.

Chapter Fourteen
A Cup of Milk

The lakeside town appears deserted, yet we wait in the woods with a good view of the road we must cross to reach it. Mazas thinks we should steer clear, but Longchamps says, "We need food. Water." For half an hour, we wait and watch. Nobody complains. We are weary, dehydrated, hungry, happy to rest.

We hear the engines before seeing the vehicles, and then four troop transports appear on the road from around a bend. Even from our distance, their make is undeniably German. As the convoy passes, we remain as motionless as boulders on the forest floor until the trucks navigate out of sight behind a turn. Longchamps says, "They've caught up with us. We'll wait another ten minutes, then if we don't see another vehicle, we'll go to the village."

Ten minutes pass too soon, and I stand on sore legs. Mazas and I stay in the rear, watching Piffet and Voulard. They both stumble down the hill as we near the road but manage to get back on their feet without help. Cows wander the pasture, ignoring our weary advance.

There is no life in the village. Windows are shuttered; the avenues deserted and dusty. Longchamps leads us toward the town center, hoping to chance upon a store not looted or a café with some crumbs left behind. Above all else, we need water. As our procession turns a corner, I see we are not alone. Three people stare at us from the other side of the plaza. Two are women, and the third is a middle-aged man who comes running to us. "What is this? Troops with no weapons? Where are your officers?"

Mazas steps forward.

"Where—" is all the man gets out when Mazas grabs him by the collar and pulls him in so their faces nearly touch.

"If only you knew!" Mazas levels his right fist. Nobody moves to stop him, but instead of striking the man, Mazas shoves him away. The man falters backward and slinks off, brushing his ruffled shirt. The two women whisper to each other but don't go to help him.

Longchamps says, "Come on, let's get out of here."

We turn to leave when one of the women runs over. She wears a headkerchief over her hair, but it slips off, so she holds it instead. "You can't stay here," she says.

"I gathered that much," Mazas declares with scorn.

"It's the Germans; they were here an hour ago. They went house to house, rounded up over a dozen soldiers in hiding. It's not safe." The young girl twists the headkerchief in her fists and repeats, "It's not safe here."

Ross replies, "We understand. Please, do you have any water, any food?"

The woman turns to the other, still reluctant to approach, and shouts for her to find something to drink.

"Is there any place for us to spend the night farther from town?" Longchamps asks. "A barn, anywhere safe?"

The woman shakes her head, a bouncy, dark hair curl escaping the tight bun. "I'm sorry, but there isn't. If the Germans return and find more soldiers—and I suspect they will return—they will burn our village to the ground. Already, they took our neighbors who harbored French soldiers. They won't hesitate to kill us all."

The second woman returns, accompanied by a third, helping her carry a milk pail. "Here," the woman says, placing the canister on the ground. "Drink."

It's hard to look away from the container as we line up and take turns dipping a tin mug into the liquid. I am fifth in line, and when given a full mug's worth, I can feel the warmth radiating from the metal cup. It must have been milked that day. As the cream soothes my throat and coats my stomach, the fats, proteins, and calories are absorbed into my bloodstream. My body shakes involuntarily, and I hand the cup to Billet behind me.

"Thank you," I say.

The pail is dry when we each drink a mug, and Piffet is given a second. We thank the women again and start to walk away. My stomach is warm, and although I don't feel as if my strength is renewed, a fog has lifted from my mind. We are close to the opposite side of town, near the lakeside, when an older gentleman appears on the road ahead. He waves, and we wave back.

"Where are you coming from?" he asks.

We tell him a rushed tale and again ask if there is a home or structure where we can spend the night. The man shakes his head and says, "No, the Germans will kill us all if they find soldiers in hiding. But I might know somewhere … do you lads have a map?"

"Yes, of course." Longchamps removes the folded map from his pocket and studies it with the man.

"There's an old barn right about …" The man's finger traces the paper. "… here or so. It belongs to the Paquet family, one town over, but the structure's been vacant for years. Falling to disrepair."

Longchamps studies the route. "Thank you," he tells the man, then turns to us. "It's a long walk, so let's move. We'll get there after nightfall."

***

We smell smoke before we see the black clouds drift to the heavens and soon hear the crackling roar of a monstrous fire. "It can't be," Brissanet says as we gather in a clearing. Hours have passed since we left the village, and whatever strength the milk provided has been worn away by the kilometers we traversed by moonlight. From our vantage, we see the massive barn consumed with fire. "No …" Brissanet says and collapses to his knees. Everyone follows suit, and soon, we are all on the ground. Cold emanates from the dirt, through my pants, and to my skin.

"Do you see anyone down there?" Longchamps asks no one in particular.

"No," Mazas replies. "You think the Germans set the fire?"

"I don't know." Longchamps is the only one standing, facing the flames with his hands on his hips. "Could have been someone else hiding in there; a cooking fire, a candle." He turns to us with exhaustion in his eyes. Defeat. Hunger. "Unroll your blankets," he says. "Get some rest. We leave at midnight to pass over the lake while it's still dark."

I echo an internal sigh of relief as I wrap my blanket over my shoulders. Far off, machine-gun fire clatters, but who knows from where. Sleep comes in slivers, seconds at a time, before noises, gunfire, or sometimes not discernable, rips me from the quiet depths. The hours go by, and despite getting no more than a moment or two of sleep, it is good not to be walking. Yet, the urge to be far from where we are outweighs comfort, and when Longchamps says, "Gear up," I am relieved. No one speaks as we roll our blankets and walk out of the thicket.

Heading straight south, we come to the water's edge. Reflected moonlight appears over the rebounding swells. The wind coming off the water is frigid and is more of a river than a lake. The mud is deep, and sometimes, my boots get stuck past my ankles. It's a chore to pull them back out. Already, my legs ache. A fire blazes from a village far behind us and another across the water, reflecting dancing flames along with the crescent moonlight. It is quiet here, other than the melodic lapping tide. The juxtaposition of beauty and destruction is hypnotic. Yet, the piercing cold dispels any enchantment. It reminds me how easy it would be to surrender our exhausted bodies and minds to the murky soil.

Chapter Fifteen
Two Bridges

The more we walk, the deeper the swampy ground becomes. First, our feet sink to the ankle and now to the calf. Twice, Voulard has fallen while trying to pry his legs from the muck, and his hands and arms are covered in thick slime. "Christ," Voulard says, "we're not going to make it out of here."

"Just a little farther," I tell him, but doubt creeps over me. My thighs are cramped from the exertion of each step, and I see a few ahead of me fall while struggling to free themselves. The cold penetrates my boots, and my pants cling to my skin, a wet, icy compress. It would be a terror to succumb to the mud, sink past the legs to the waist, unable to escape the sludge's confines and drown in a frigid mire. I've heard stories from the last war of men drowning in the craters of no man's land. What a horrible fate.

"This is hell," Voulard says, and I can't help but agree.

Longchamps leads the procession and calls back, "The ground is firm here."

"Thank God," Voulard says.

We reach solid ground one by one, and everyone is exhausted. Mud is plastered inside my boots.

"You led us the wrong way," someone says to Longchamps. I turn to see Chanal removing his backpack and sitting on it. "There must have been an easier route."

Longchamps doesn't reply.

Mazas faces Chanal. "How would any of us know where the ground is swamp and where it is not?"

Chanal lights a cigarette and doesn't answer. But Mazas is irritated and continues, "We made it, didn't we? Nobody died, huh? Suck it up."

Chanal takes a large inhale and looks down as he exhales. "I'm just exhausted is all," he says.

"No shit."

"All right," Longchamps cuts in. "We can't sit around. We'll freeze."

We proceed again into the woods, but the ground remains firm. Small branches whip at my face, and thorny brush snags my clothing. The mud on my pants is ice-cold and soaked through to my skin. God, I want to be away from this lakeside. If only we could stop for an hour somewhere indoors and have a fire to dry our clothes and warm our bodies and spirits.

When Brissanet says, "There ahead … is that a bridge?" hope bursts in my chest. The water is wide here, and from where we walk, I see the side of a concrete structure jutting from the water's edge. It must be a bridge.

We are fast to a rutted dirt road where the ground inclines, and we follow it to a trench separating us from the abutment where the bridge begins. "The roadway is missing," Longchamps says, looking around in the dark as if he'll discover the missing portion.

Judging by the imprinted dirt lane leading to the bridge, this road was used by local farmers and civilians. Otherwise, it would have been paved. We line up along the edge of the trench, looking across the gap to the opposite jutted-out bridge portion, appearing to be almost two meters wide. The fall is roughly the same. "I'll go first," Longchamps says and steps back to have a running start. He removes his gear, squats in a runner's stance before taking off, and leaps across the divide. He makes it close to the embankment but falls short. "Shit!" he shouts from inside the trench. I see he's sunk down to his knees in swampy mud.

"Hold on, I'm coming," Mazas says.

"No, wait." Longchamps struggles to step forward and grab ahold of the rim of the abutment, but he manages to hoist himself up and out of the muck.

We all strip off our gear, and one by one, we run and leap over. Half of us land the jump. The other half wade through the slime. I'm last and heave the gear left behind across the ditch. "Christ," I mutter as I pick up a backpack. My biceps and shoulders are sore, but I don't pause until every bag is thrown over. Finally, it's my turn to jump. I walk back a distance to get as much speed as possible, but like most others, I land shy.

"Shit!" I yell. The mud is a thin, cold porridge, and the wetness is absorbed fast into my pants and spreads upward. I wade to the opposite wall and reach up to the waiting hands to be pulled free of the miserable ooze.

"This is hell," Voulard repeats. No one says otherwise.

Everyone is turned to the lake, staring out … the large bridge that crossed the river has been demolished. The structure juts out over the tide for several meters, then ends abruptly. It's too dark, and the lake too wide to see the opposite shore. Boulders of roadway and massive cement blocks emerge from the rapids.

"The water must be shallow," Mazas says. "The cement sections aren't drowned."

Clouds have rolled in, and the moonlight is gone. Making out the half-submerged structure is difficult, but it looks navigable.

"Okay," Longchamps says. "Zenner, take point." Longchamp has confessed to me that he's not a strong swimmer.

I nod and begin to the shoreline. Having the men follow me is strange, and I feel the weight of responsibility heavy on my shoulders. The cement blocks form something of a pathway, and I step out to the first boulder. It is firm and not too slippery. The water froths around me as I go from one block to another. Halfway across, fires become visible far in the distance, and the noise of the water drowns out the men's boots clomping from one cement portion to the next.

Once I reach the opposite shore, I drop my backpack and turn to help Longchamps, who followed my lead. "Go help Mazas," he says with labored breaths. I don't hesitate to return to the rocks to reach Mazas, who is holding both his gear and Voulard's. I take Voulard's bag and bring it to the shore. Piffet manages across without any aid. I respect him then, realizing he rarely asks for help despite his hardship.

Once we're gathered, there is a collective sigh of relief. Many had slipped into the water and are soaked and miserable. Voulard fell twice and might have been swept off by the current if Mazas hadn't been there to grab ahold of him. I continue to take the lead, and we come to a terrible surprise: this piece of land is narrow, and the bridge comprises two sections. We are standing on an island, and opposite, the second arch lies in ruin. We have to cross a second time.

Chapter Sixteen
Dusty Water

Crossing the rubble of the second bridge takes an hour, and once on the other side, Voulard has to sit and catch his breath. Piffet shows remarkable willpower and does not join him. After recouping for a few minutes, we continue in a single file. As we near the first intersection, Mazas warns, "Keep your eyes open."

After a few more steps, Longchamps whispers, "Take a knee," and motions for us all to drop down. "I'll scout ahead with Mazas. Everyone else, wait here." Before anyone can respond, shadows envelop their departure.

Brissanet leans close to my ear and whispers, "What will we do if Germans guard the entrance to the road?"

"I don't know," I say. "Find another way, I guess."

During the rigorous crossing, I forgot about my thirst, but now it's back, gripping my throat in raw distress. I hear Voulard complain behind me, along with someone else, Weber. We are close to starvation, but thirst has us near tears. That and the cold. We are soaked, our clothing saturated in fetid-smelling murk.

Shadowy shapes emerge as Longchamps and Mazas return. "It's clear," Longchamps says. "A sign ahead says we're in Malbuisson."

"Thank God," Brissanet whispers and lets out a long exhale. "Let's get the hell out of here."

My pant legs have stiffened and creak as we walk, with flakes of muck falling away. My throat feels like it will crack open like desert ground, and nobody speaks as we hike an elevated path. We take to the woods in the dark, following Longchamps, and soon, the trees lessen, and we walk onto a grassy field.

"Let's stop," Longchamps says. "At daybreak, we'll look for water."

Nobody argues. As we drop our gear and remove our blankets, someone says, "You hear that?" I strain to listen, and Mazas tells everyone to hush, though nobody speaks. Then I hear chiming. Cowbells.

"Anyone know how to milk a cow?" Longchamps asks.

Brissanet answers, "How hard can it be?"

Chanal and Maligeay speak up. "I grew up on a farm," Chanal says. Maligeay says the same, and they take off with five others. I also grew up on a farm, but we never owned animals larger than sheep.

"Christ, I hope they get some milk," I say to Mazas. "My throat feels like it's bleeding."

"Mine too," he responds.

The cold emanates from the ground, through the blanket and my clothing, and I'm shaking. The bones in my body rattle uncontrollably. Then I hear laughter in the distance. "They found the cows," I say. "Thank God."

It takes a while until they return. "It wasn't easy," Chanal tells us. "We got what we could." They have three canteens full of warm, smooth milk. Everyone has their tin cups waiting, and they portion out the liquid. A sigh of relief releases from us all as the milk is drained back in fast gulps, and the warmth spreads from my stomach to my legs, feet, and hands. The burning in my throat is soothed, and all at once, I am tired. I lay out, but again, the cold penetrates my clothing, and the ground is wet enough that frigid water creeps through my blanket and uniform.

"This is the devil," Brissanet says. "This is hell." His voice is shaky.

One by one, we stand and move around, trying to keep warm, and after an hour, Longchamps says, "We need to keep moving. We'll freeze to death."

"I agree," Mazas replies, and everyone nods their acceptance, even Voulard.

We pack up and start walking. It does little to warm me up, even with my blanket draped over my shoulders, but it's better than lying on the wet ground.

"We need to find food," Brissanet tells me. "My stomach is killing me."

"Mine too." The milk feels as if it absorbed into my body the moment it passed my lips, and its fortifying effects have dissipated.

Something touches my hair, and I bat my hand, swatting away whatever fly or bug is up there. My palm returns wet, and I look at the dark sky and feel another droplet and then another. All heads crane upward.

"It's raining," someone says.

"Just a drizzle." Mazas sticks his tongue out to collect droplets.

Then, all at once, it comes down in plummeting beads.

"Follow me," Longchamps shouts and runs ahead to a group of trees. We gather at the bases, though the boughs do little to shield the droplets. Soon, water drips down my face from my soaked hair. Lightning flashes in the distance.

An idea strikes me, and I remove my backpack and go through my gear.

"What are you doing?" Mazas asks.

"Watch," I say and fold up a section of map into a funnel. Then I unscrew the top of my canteen and hold it under a branch. "Weber, shake it."

He reaches out and shakes the branch; sure enough, my canteen fills. Everyone begins doing the same. Weber is searching his bag for a map when he says, "Look at this!" He holds out a tin of sardines. "I didn't know I had it!"

"This is a miracle," Brissanet says and takes a long pull of cold water. I do the same. It tastes dusty, yet it's delicious all the same.

Weber opens the tin and uses his knife to cut the thin fish into smaller sections, and we each get a morsel of meat. Fats and proteins explode on my tongue, and I'm not sure if I've ever tasted anything quite as good.

After drinking my fill, I pack my canteen, and we all lean against each other, trying to stay warm. The rain slows to a drizzle, and Longchamps asks us each how we are. Everyone is freezing. Everyone is hungry. But at least we have water. "It's five a.m.," he says. "Let's move. We can't stay still, wet and cold like this."

A thin crack in the cloud cover displays a rising sun high in the heavens.

"Switzerland must be close," Mazas tells me. "It must be."

A few yards further, Voulard pauses. "Hey, look there." He leans over and delicately cuts a flower from the stem. We stop and examine the flower patch. Each blossom holds a few sips of rainwater inside its bright petals. I reach down and pick one, sipping the sweet water. Brissanet does the same, then puts the entire flower in his mouth and chews.

"Any good?" I ask.

He makes a sour expression and spits it out. "The petals aren't bad, but the stem is bitter."

The sky clears as we walk on, yet it remains cold. I take the lead with Longchamps, and he says, "At least it's beautiful here."

I agree, although I am so tired and hungry that I didn't take much heed.

Then he says, "There's a tub ahead," and points. Sure enough, there's a rectangular stone in a clearing. We walk to it. "Must be for cows."

"If I see one," Brissanet says, "I'll slaughter it myself. We should have killed those last cows we milked. We need to eat."

Everyone looks, but no cows are in sight, no bells ringing. Longchamps reaches into the tub and scoops up a palmful of water. "It's clean," he says. "And cold." We fill our canteens again and drink straight from the tub. I splash some water over my face, but it's frigid.

We continue the march up and around a cluster of shallow hills and arrive at a modest village dimpled in the low of a valley. A street marker reads: *Longeville*. The homes are deserted, and we go from one to the other, searching for anything edible. Mazas and I approach a house, and I feel reluctance, knowing that I am breaking into someone's home, intruding upon their life. Yet, hunger propels me, and we enter without further pause. The house is unassuming and opens to a joint living room and kitchen. Mazas goes to the cabinets, and I follow. "Please, God," he says, and we open one after another. There is nothing. Not even a bag of flour or grain.

Mazas and I continue to other buildings, but don't find anything. The homes smell like life, warmth, a thousand cooked meals, perfumes, and soaps. They make me sad, and I tell Mazas, "It's no use." Still, we check two more homes before reconvening with the group.

"Well?" Mazas asks Longchamps as we approach. "Any luck?"

"Half a loaf of rock-hard bread," Longchamps says, "and some sugar cubes."

The sugar cubes are passed out as we walk, and I let them soak onto my tongue and disintegrate. It is now late afternoon, and the sun has dried me off a bit. A road becomes visible through the brush and Longchamps motions for us to stop. "Everyone else, hold up. Zenner, come with me."

I follow Longchamps into a thicket of bushes, prowling closer until we have a fair vantage of the road and can see a village much like the last.

"You think it's safe?" I ask.

Longchamps doesn't reply. He stares ahead and then says, "I don't see movement, but that doesn't mean it's empty. Plus, the road is wide, and it's daylight. Crossing now is dangerous."

I nod.

Longchamps is saying, "Let's give it a half an—" when the unmistakable noise of engines cuts his words short. We lower ourselves in the brush until we are lying flat, and it doesn't take long until two, three, and then four vehicles appear on the road a hundred yards from where we hide. A convoy of German transports pass and continue on their way. We don't speak. We don't move. A second convoy passes, five or six vehicles, the backs loaded with troops. Three trucks stop on the side of the road, and the troops jump out. I can hear them speaking, shouting orders, and the soldiers stretch their backs and yawn. Another convoy rumbles by as the soldiers on the ground disappear into the village with their MP 40s and MG 42s. I look at Longchamps, and he looks at me; then we both watch the Germans enter the town.

Chapter Seventeen
The Mountains

The last thing I ate was stale bread and two sugar cubes; now, we are out of food. The day is warm, and we backpedaled far enough away from the road where we saw the German convoy that we feel comfortable letting our guards down a bit. Everyone unrolls their blankets to dry in the sun, and those of us with a pair of socks change them. It feels marvelous to peel away the soaked, muddy wool covering my blistered and bleeding heels and wear a new, warm pair. If only we had a fire to thaw our feet.

Conversation is minimal and whispered. Most of us use the time to close our eyes. Finally, we are dry, and the sun is pleasant. I write in my journal, recalling everything I can of the towns and woods we've passed since the last opportunity I had to write. As I explain my hunger in the journal, I can't help but recall how strong and well-fed I was before this mess of a war. An athlete. Back in Paris, back in another life, my ambitions were high. A phantom concept that I might one day perform again for a crowd and daydream of making it to the big times, in Medrano Circus or the d'Hiver. I was destined for more than this. My mind and body; what a shame if I should perish on this mountainside.

Three cigarettes dwindle to ash as I pass the time, and soon, my eyes grow weary. The sleep following is short yet so deep that when I wake to hear the rumbling of a convoy on the distant highway, it takes a moment to process my surroundings. My watch shows that an hour has passed. It's the longest stretch of sleep I've had in days, and it feels marvelous, yet not enough.

Sleep comes again in short intervals, but as the sun sets, the cold returns.

At nine at night, Longchamps stands and stretches. "I'll check the road," he says. I'm about to volunteer to go along, but Mazas quickly steps forward, and they walk off into the woods.

"Can I borrow your lighter?" Brissanet asks. "Mine's run dry."

I hand him my lighter and then use it to light my own cigarette. Longchamps and Mazas return. "Let's go," Longchamps says. "The road is quiet."

We stretch before putting on our packs, then follow Longchamps into the brush. We pause by the roadside, listening for any disturbances, and try to glimpse the distant town bathed in moonlight, then walk fast across the significant avenue. Deserted or not, my heart beats hard with trepidation, knowing that German convoys could return at any moment. Even though none of us are armed with anything other than utility knives, there's a good chance we'd be shot on sight without provocation if caught.

We veer around the village to the hills behind. The moonlight boasts massive mountains in the cool, clear night, and it's challenging to decipher the true scope of their peaks. The gentle harmony of flowing water leads to a small brook at the base of the ascent. The water is easy to cross by stepping on large stones, with the moonlight reflecting along the ripples, and Ross behind me says, "This must be where the Doubs begins."

A few yards after the brook, we face the climb, which is far steeper than the distant view made us believe. "The way I see it," Longchamps says, "there are two ways to go about this. We can stay on our current path, which looks to snake up and along the hills. The second option is to climb straight up. It won't be easy, but it will be quicker and a sure way over."

No one offers their opinion, and Longchamps takes that as agreement. "Over it is then. Take a moment to drink." He goes from one man to the next as we sip from our canteens, ensuring everyone is prepared for the climb. When he reaches Brissanet and myself, he whispers, "I need you two to stay in the rear with Voulard. He's not doing well. Mazas will keep an eye on Piffet."

We agree, and Longchamps continues, "I overheard Voulard telling Billet that he wants to quit. He wants to go back to the town we passed and give up. He'll be captured for sure, and if he is, the Germans will know our direction."

"I won't let that happen," Brissanet says. "I'll roll him up and over the damn mountain if it comes to it."

"It's not the poor guy's fault. He's beyond exhausted."

"We all are."

"Not like him. What if he faints on the trek ahead? Or worse, his heart could trouble him; remember, none of us are doctors."

"You can count on us," I tell Longchamps.

"I know," he says and walks off.

We pack our canteens and start the incline. The mountain is covered in pine trees, and it doesn't take long for the canopy of branches to blur out the moonlight. There is no path to follow, and Longchamps leads us straight into the darkness.

"Son of a bitch," Brissanet says, rubbing his cheek. "These damn things are sharp."

The incline worsens, and my pack's weight feels like it is growing.

"I can't …" Voulard says and drops to his hands and knees to propel himself around boulders half-buried in the frozen ground. "It's … I can't …"

I'm out of breath but mutter, "Give me your pack."

We stop for a moment, leaning against pine trees for support, and Brissanet rummages through Voulard's possessions, splitting up what we can fit in our own backpacks. "Here," he says, passing it back to Voulard. "It's nearly empty." I can smell the large man perspiring and even feel the heat emanating from his body. Voulard turns back to the procession, of which we are the last, and continues. Brissanet and I follow. A branch whips out of nowhere, caught first on Voulard's gear, and wallops against my face.

"Son of a bitch," I say, feeling a hot trickle high on my left cheek. I touch my face, and my fingers come away wet. "I'm going to lose an eye before getting out of here."

"I can't imagine Longchamps is having an easy go in the lead," Brissanet tells me.

The incline sharpens, and I sometimes drop to my hands and knees, grabbing patches of grass and half-submerged rocks to pull myself onward. A desire to lie down on the cold earth, with sleep attempting to rein me in, to overtake my strength. My eyes want to shut; they do shut and are forced back open.

"Hold up," Longchamps shouts in a ragged voice. As we take a break, I lean against a tree, fighting the urge to slumber in the cold. The wind filters through my uniform, permeates the rips and tears, turning my sweat-soaked body into an icy frost.

"Okay," Longchamp says in a hoarse voice. "We have to keep moving."

The group lurches upward. The trees thin, yet the low brush thickens. The incline is so sharp that I can't stand straight but must remain on my hands and knees. It looks as if we are crawling straight to the bright moon and stars above. Voulard is speaking, but I don't know what he says. I can't respond. Each gust of cold wind feels as if it will strike me off the face of the mountain and send me flying into the abyss, like a dog shaking fleas from its fur.

I stop.

My cheek touches the ground, turning the soil to mud against the sweat, but I push myself back to my hands and knees. Vision strobes white, and I'm afraid I'm going to faint. I must have spoken my fears out loud because Mazas is at my side, also on his hands and knees, and he grabs my elbow and pulls me onward. "You're not going to faint," he says in an exhausted huff. "I've got you."

It's not long until we stop again. A voice says, "We have to keep going." I open my eyes and see Weber talking to Longchamps. Half the group is catatonic, fighting the pull of sleep, the urge to close our eyes and let the cold earth turn us into frozen corpses high in the mountains, to be lost until some hikers find us by chance if this terrible war ever ends. "We can't stop," Weber says.

"You're right," Longchamps agrees. "Let's go."

The incline becomes steeper, and the grass is wet. I look up to see everyone crawling, and then my arms give out, and my face hits the ground. Mazas is fast to grab my shoulder. "Get up." His voice is wavering. He takes my backpack, and I protest. But Mazas says, "Keep going."

"Vou-Voulard," I say, turning to see Voulard being pushed along by Brissanet. "I'm s-so sorry, Mazas." My vision strobes bright white, the peripherals dark. In a flash, my mind wanders back to the crossing at Port-sur-Saône. There's something about the last thing I saw before crossing while I cried out loud beside the old woman with the bad knees. When I looked down, someone had left their birdcage behind, the caged door open, the bird gone. Free. How lucky, that bird without a cage, to fly free of this nightmare. A euphoria overtakes me, wishing I, too, could soar into the heavens and find peace in the clouds.

"Just keep going," Mazas says, snapping me out of my fantasy. "We're almost there."

"H-how do you know?"

"I don't."

Five minutes later, we break again, but only to catch our breath. Longchamps is pale and leans against a tree. His breathing is labored, and he almost slips from the tree but catches himself.

"I'll take the lead," Ross says.

Longchamps nods, and we continue. My numb fingers can't grab hold of the slippery ground. "I'm so tired," I say. "I … I can't keep my eyes open."

Mazas doesn't reply, but he pushes his shoulder into the back of my thigh, propelling me onward. A few yards further, Ross calls back, "Careful ahead." A low, aged stone wall stretches before us, seemingly part of an old farm. The top is lined with rusted barbed wire. Ross cuts the wire and peels it back, and one by one, we step over.

The wind is slowing, and Brissanet tells us, "I think we've reached the summit."

"Thank God," I mutter.

"Just a little further," Longchamps adds, retaking lead alongside Ross.

The ground levels, and I can stand.

"I'm so sorry, Mazas. I've never …"

"We're all exhausted," he says. "We're starving. You have nothing to be ashamed of."

But I am. Longchamps depended on me to help Voulard, but instead, I was the one who needed help, and Brissanet was left alone. Piffet was pushed on by Weber since Mazas had to tend to me. The shame is deep, worsened by the hunger pangs and terrible weariness.

"Every part of my body aches," Mazas says. I think he is trying to make me feel better, but instead, I feel worse, knowing I have added to his misery.

I'm in the back of the group, with only Voulard and Piffet behind me. Mazas, Brissanet, and Weber are with us, and I'm ashamed to be so incapable. Now that the ground is balanced, a degree of strength has returned, but still, just walking is arduous, and my toes seem to strike every stone on the trail. It is midnight now, and the moon projects long shadows from the pine trees.

I wonder when we'll begin the descent, but Longchamps calls out, "Let's stop here. The wind isn't so bad."

Nobody protests. Nestled in my blanket, the cold ground welcomes me to weary slumber.

Chapter Eighteen
Wednesday, 19 June, 1940

Five of us are missing blankets. Most likely snagged away by tree branches during the climb, from where they were kept rolled up on the top of our backpacks. Wind cuts across the plateau like cold blades piercing our uniforms. Minutes after closing my eyes, I am stirred by Brissanet. "Can I share your blanket?" His arms are clutched across his chest. We huddle on the frigid ground, stretching the blanket to cover us both. Now that we're not moving, the bitter temperature is freezing my uniform against my skin. Wet from perspiration, mud, and filth. After a moment, Brissanet snores, and I mutter, "At least one of us can sleep."

The cold gusts don't diminish but continue like a fan turned on high, penetrating the wool blanket. I rub my palms together, curl up, and put my hands between my knees. Nothing can stop the shaking from deep within my core, made worse by terrible fatigue. "Damn wind," I say to myself and get up and maneuver mine and Brissanet's bags to shield us, to little avail. The breeze gets around and over, no matter how I stack them. Somehow, Brissanet is sleeping hard, his snoring deep and guttural.

"It's no use. No fucking use." I get up again, leaving Brissanet under my blanket, and see Piffet's eyes open. I cross my arms, trembling, and ask, "Can I share your blanket?" The cuts on my face from the pine boughs howl in pain with each gust.

"Of course," he says.

I first maneuver his bag to act as a shield and lie down. Piffet's body is warmer under the blanket than Brissanet's, and my mind skirts on the border of reality and fantasy, so close to dreams. My side against the ground is numb, and the cold wind pierces the other side. Sleep is not possible.

Longchamps' voice cuts the quiet. "All right," he says and clears weariness from his throat. "We have to continue. We'll die if we stay any longer. Come on, all of you. Wake up. Let's move."

Everyone is quick to stand, except Brissanet, who I imagine is the only one who could sleep in this icebox. "What time is it?" Piffet asks while rolling up his blanket.

Squinting in the dim moonlight, I say, "A quarter after two."

Longchamps shoulders his backpack but then falters and grabs the side of a pine tree for support. "You all right?" I ask, stepping to him.

"Yeah," he says before turning into the shadows for us to follow. I stay close behind, and more than once, he fumbles over rocks or a branch. He stops every now and again, looking around in the darkness, and we follow … the weary leading the weary.

"Shit," Longchamps says, and stumbles. Mazas and I rush to his side as he falls to his hands and knees. "My ankle's caught."

His foot is shrouded in darkness, caught on something. He yanks until it breaks free. The sharp points of discarded barbed wire are candescent in the moonlight, twisted along the ground. "You okay?" I ask.

"Fine." He stands on wobbly legs and calls, "Careful of your footing."

Ross approaches from the rear. "I can take point."

I'm glad he volunteers. I know I cannot lead, and Longchamps looks ill. He relents without protest, and Ross navigates us down the side of the mountain, where the ground is spongy underfoot. "Watch yourselves," he says as we pass another low stone wall lined with barbed wire strung from ancient wooden posts.

It's not difficult to step over, but several of us get snagged.

"Shit," I hear, and turn to see Piffet pull his jacket free from a spike with an audible rip. "Damn thing cut me!"

As if sleepwalking, we descend the mountain, tripping, falling, cursing, but the wind lessens the farther we go. We come to another brick wall lined with barbed wire and hold up as Ross cuts it away. When we all step over the crudely stacked stones, Longchamps says, "It's warm enough to sleep here. We can't … I can't go any further. We need rest."

"Thank God," I say to no one. Mazas hears me and nods.

We line up against the wall and remove our blankets, sharing them to form one long line of a huddled mass. There is no wind, and I close my eyes to be transported quickly into the void of dreamless worlds.

***

The sky is clear, and a sunray is cast upon my cheek. Never have I felt such comfort. Warmth, in all its limitations high up on that mountain, thaws life into my chilled skin. Mazas remains under the blanket, his side going up and down with each breath. It is nine in the morning when I stand and stretch. Most of us are awake, and Longchamps nods when he sees me. I walk off to pee against the side of a tree, but only a trickle comes out. Again, thirst grips my throat, and I take the last two sips of water left in my canteen. Everyone has laid their blankets out in the sun to dry, and I do the same. Then, I take a seat on the grass beside Longchamps.

"You sleep?" he asks.

"Yes. Better than I have since ... well, I don't know."

He nods. "Me too. If we didn't stop when we did, I think I would have fainted."

"You're not the only one. Thank God the wind is shielded here. Another night without sleep, and we'd all be sick."

He finds his open pack of cigarettes and offers them out to whoever isn't already smoking. I accept and smoke, realizing for the first time since we began our climb how beautiful it is here. The trees are a healthy, vibrant green with shades of red and brown.

"Is there any water nearby?" I ask the group. Everyone either shrugs or says no. After I finish my cigarette, I say, "I'll backtrack a short way. The ground was soft on the trail last night; maybe there's a spring."

"Good thinking," Longchamps says and lies on the plush grass. His face is pale where it isn't covered in grime. Here, we have warmth and distance from the German invaders. If at least for a short while, we need comfort and absorb the sun like withered plants. It's not easy to stand and begin walking, and I fear that some of us won't make it much farther without food and water. These woods will become our tomb—not the worst place to die, considering the options.

However, I will not give up so easily or let anyone in our group do the same. As long as I have the strength to stand, I will do whatever I can to find food, water—anything to help. I owe it to everyone after my humiliating climb up the mountain when I discovered how close and easy dying can be.

As I step over the stone wall, Mazas stirs, shoots up, and looks around. "Where—" His words are cut short by a cough. After seeing everyone awake, he clears his throat and lies back down, closing his eyes against the bright sun.

The woods open up to rolling grass hills, wavering ever so slightly. The far horizon is crisp and blue, a perfect canvas of an immaculate sky. Standing where I believe I felt the spongy ground, I don't see any indication of water. Still, I look over the plateau. Tears want to arrive, both in awe of the surroundings and because this is the first time I'm alone with my thoughts in days. The last time I had privacy was back in Sarrebourg. That could have been a different life. Back then, despite knowing the Germans were in northern France, largely avoiding the Maginot Line and that their soldiers were fierce, a degree of hope was held that all was not lost. Even when we fled in our trucks, I was confident that we would be safe and France would not fall. But it did. And so quickly.

I turn from that stunning vista, unable to shed a tear, and join my friends, my fellow soldiers. Longchamps's eyes are shut, and he might be sleeping as I lean against a nearby tree. Those of us awake are quiet. Ross and Weber play cards, and I remove my journal and write about last night's experience. The ink has smeared in places already written, but it's still legible.

We must leave this place soon, but nobody is eager to go. Most of us remain lying down, eyes closed. Half an hour passes when Brissanet says, "I'm going to look for water, food."

"I'll join you," I say, and we walk into the woods. We travel east in a circular pattern, stopping at vantage points and open plains.

"You think it's strange that we haven't seen any animals?" Brissanet asks.

"I suppose so. I know nothing about these woods or what animals should live here."

Brissanet looks at me. "It's the woods. There should be animals."

I agree with him, and we continue in a loop back toward the clearing. Then I hear something. "Hey, listen." The sound is unmistakable. Cowbells. We walk toward the noise and soon hear more bells. When we step through a cluster of bushes, a field opens up, and we see them. Twenty or more cows grazing in a field.

"Thank the Lord." Brissanet looks skyward and kisses a rosary hanging from his neck. "Milk. Meat."

"Look." I point down in the valley, far in the corner. "The field is plowed. There must be a farm nearby. Come, let's tell the others."

Brissanet pauses, staring at the cows.

"If there is a farm," I say, "we will ask before taking."

"And if they won't give us anything?"

"We'll figure it out. But we'll eat and have milk, one way or the other."

Reluctantly, Brissanet turns and says, "Okay."

We walk quickly back to the group, running at times, but become too lightheaded for long stretches. "There are cows," I blurt out, surprising everyone. "Not far."

Ross's eyes shoot wide, and he is fast to his feet. "We must eat," he says. "Take me there."

Longchamps sits up and says, "You three, go. Bring enough canteens so we can all drink."

All eyes are upon us as we go back into the woods. Pleading, starving stares.

"Is there a farmhouse?" Ross asks.

"We didn't see one, but there must be. A field at the bottom of the pasture is plowed; the soil looks freshly turned over."

We step around the same thick brush, and Ross visibly trembles at seeing the cows. His mouth widens into a smile. "Come on," he says, and the three of us begin crossing the meadow. A clear line of shorter, grazed grass follows a barbed-wire fence, which continues into the far woods and is lost from sight.

"Down there." I point to the plowed field. "There's a building. Two buildings."

"Are those horses?" Ross asks.

I squint. "I think so."

"Someone must be home."

The grassy field is covered in deep depressions from the cow's hooves. When we get close to the home, we see the door is ajar, and a dog comes running out without barking. Its long tongue bounces out the side of its mouth.

"We're not going to hurt you!" Ross yells at the house. "We are hungry—starving! All we want is some milk!"

The door remains shut. The dog's tail is in a frenzy, and the mutt goes from one of us to the next and then back again, licking our hands. "Please!" Ross yells and leans against a long, weathered table in the yard. I walk around back to the open barn door. Inside are stacks of hay and the barnyard sound of animals in pens. There is a creaking noise behind me as the home's rear door opens, and a woman stands on the porch looking at me. I open my mouth to speak, but words are stuck on my lips. The woman's brown hair is up in a headkerchief, and her face is lined by years of hard work, yet she does not appear over forty. Her eyes pierce me; her stoic expression is striking, her arms crossed before her frayed blue shirt. Again, I try to speak, but all that comes out is, "Ross!"

He appears around the side of the home with Brissanet, says, "Please," and holds his hands before him in prayer. "Can you spare anything to eat? We've been traveling for days. We are starving."

Her stern demeanor cracks, and she steps toward us, wiping her palms against an apron. "Yes," she says. "I have plenty."

"There are more of us," I add.

"How many?"

"Eighteen."

She nods, seeming to make a quick calculation, and tells us, "Go get them. We'll milk some cows, and I have plenty of cheese and potatoes. You're soldiers?"

For a moment, we are entranced, staring at this woman, our savior. "Yes," Brissanet says, his eyes wet.

"Follow me," she says, and we walk to the barn. She takes a pail from where it hangs from a peg in the wall and enters a stall where a cow is contently chewing on hay. She sits on a stool and begins milking with skill and ease. After a few pumps, she picks up the bucket. "Here. Drink."

Ross takes a slow sip, his eyes closing, and then passes Brissanet the pail. When it reaches me, I don't hesitate. The warm milk surges down my throat, easing the dryness, the fats bursting on my tongue.

I hand her the pail. "I …" I say. "I don't know how to thank you." With that, I start crying, as do Ross and Brissanet.

The woman continues milking the cow and tells us, "My family left to fight. It's been weeks since I've heard from any of them, my husband and two sons. I'm alone here. There is too much for one person to do. Too many cows to milk, too many seeds to plant." The milk comes out in long spurts, making a clang as it hits the wall of the pail. "Go get the others," she says.

"I'll go," I say, overwhelmed by our luck and by the generosity we've encountered. Feeling encouraged, I run across the field. All the while, the little dog follows me. I stop in front of the fence and scratch behind his shaggy ears, thinking he should stay. His belly and chest are white fur, but his back and most of his face are dark brown. I step over the fence, and the dog follows, finding a path he looks accustomed to taking. This is a good place to be a dog, high in the mountains, with freedom to explore. No fear of war. No worry of starvation. Better to be a dog than a man.

I run to where the meadow meets the woods and continue toward the clearing. There is noise ahead, and I imagine it's our men, but then I halt in front of a different procession. My heart thumps, thinking that the Germans have found us, but their uniforms are French, and they are heading in a reversed path from our own. They see me, and one calls out, "Hello!"

"Hello," I reply. "Where are you going?"

"Grenoble," one says. They are about a dozen, healthy-looking, not as dirty and disheveled as our group.

"Grenoble? That's, what … two hundred kilometers from here?"

"We've been told it's safe there."

I shake my head. "It's not."

They look to one another, uncertain, but maintain, "We have orders."

"You'll walk straight into the Germans the way you're going. The Swiss border is close; you can come with us."

They don't have a good reply. Just go on about orders. I wish them well, and they continue on their way. The clearing isn't far, and I jog the rest of the way until coming to a halt in front of the men. I'm out of breath but manage to say, "There's a farm … a farmer. Plenty of food."

Half the men shed tears from raw, red eyes, and Voulard needs help getting to his feet. Longchamps stands, and the color drains from his face as he falters, but he gathers himself. "Come," I say and lead them to the pasture and the farmhouse at the base of the meadow.

Chapter Nineteen
The Farm

Our weary assemblage arrives as the farmer places a stack of plates on the wooden table in front of the home. Large milk containers are filled to the brim, and we drink fervently. A second woman is with the first, and she tells me, "I live on a neighboring farm. We both have too many cows to milk, and the animals are starting to get sick. Please, drink all that you can."

"You're a saint," I tell her.

"We have potatoes cooking, but the Germans are in Longeville and could come this way, so please; there is a wooded area across the field. Take the milk and plates. We'll bring the potatoes to you when they're ready."

We're led to a clearing in a patch of woods, carrying what's left of the milk and a whole wheel of firm cheese. Already, color is returning to our faces, and Voulard walks with regained strength.

"I can't believe the luck," Longchamps says. He cuts the cheese into wedges and hands them out. The women return, making two trips and leaving us with four pots of food. Steam billows out when the tops are removed, and the vapors of potatoes stewed in butter envelop my senses. Portions are doled onto each plate, and my teeth crunch against a salt crystal on the first bite and sink into the creamy potato. "I've never," I say while chewing, "tasted anything so good."

The women return again, carrying three bottles of wine. "It's all we have," the farmer says.

"It's more than enough," Longchamps tells her. We all agree, thanking them, praising their generosity. A full meal, more milk than we can drink in one sitting, and even some wine.

"I will never have a finer meal," I say.

"Don't be silly," the woman tells me. "Just eat. Stay in the woods until it's dark, just in case. You can sleep in the barn if there's no sign of the Germans after nightfall."

We thank them again, and they leave.

Voulard sighs audibly and lies back, using his backpack as a pillow. Sitting beside me, Longchamps whispers, "It's good to see him smile again. It's good to see everyone smile."

I nod. "My stomach is so full I'm in pain."

The meal puts most of us to sleep, but I stay awake, writing in my journal and smoking cigarettes. By seven o'clock, the sun is declining, and weariness sinks in. Longchamps studies a map with Mazas and says, "There isn't a highway for kilometers around. The chances of German infantry coming in the night are slim to none. I think it's safe to go to the barn."

"I agree," Mazas says.

"All right then," Longchamps addresses the group, waking more than a few up. "Let's get going."

There is a lantern inside the barn on an empty wine barrel, but when Weber strikes a match to the wick, Longchamps tells him, "No light."

I find a spot in the hay and form it into a soft mattress. When I close my eyes, sleep arrives on swift wings.

***

I am awake before dawn but stay wrapped in my blanket, allowing my body to absorb comfort for as long as possible. My arms and legs tingle, and every muscle aches, yet I feel better than I have in days. Cigarette smoke lingers in the air, along with muffled voices. When it becomes evident that everyone is getting up and packing their gear, I do the same. Mazas is rolling up his blanket and asking me, "Do you believe in fate?"

"What do you mean?"

"Fate. Do you think fate brought us here, to this farm?"

"I don't know. Probably luck."

"Maybe luck and fate are one and the same."

"How can that be? Fate is a predetermined course or circumstance. Luck, well, it's just that. Luck. It's chance."

Mazas makes a clicking sound in his mouth, then pulls a cigarette from the pack. He offers me one. "Perhaps." He holds out a light. "But doesn't it seem fortunate that after a string of miserable, cold nights, after we climb a mountain, run out of food and water, skirt so close to serious injury and death, we find this place in the middle of nowhere? An oasis."

"Are you saying that this is all predetermined? That we were meant to find this farm?"

He shrugs. "Maybe."

"Then what about France falling to the Germans? Was that also predetermined?"

"No," he says and takes a deep inhale. "That was stupidity on the part of the government for not fortifying our defenses at the Belgian border."

I laugh. "How can one thing be fate and not the other?"

He laughs along with me. "Beats me," he says, and we both stand and join Longchamps at the barn door. It's a cool morning, and a wispy fog hugs the ground as the dew evaporates in the developing daylight.

"It's a quarter to six," Longchamps says. "We move out in fifteen minutes."

We both nod, then look to the farmhouse as the back door creaks open. The dog darts out, licking and sniffing one man and then the next. It is great to see everyone smile at the floppy-eared animal, scratch its head, finding pleasure in the dog's simple delight. Both women appear at the door and walk over with full milk pails. "They're still warm," we're told. "Drink up."

The milk is delicious, laden with fat and protein. Everyone has a long drink and then fills their canteens. Longchamps tells us it's time to go. One by one, we thank the two farmers, standing in a line to hug them each. Ross and Brissanet shed tears, thanking them for their kindness, and a lump forms in my throat as I say goodbye. They smell of the earth, soil, sage, and a sweet, floral scent, like wildflowers and lavender. Ross hands them both a thick fold of money before we go. They refuse at first but then take it when he insists.

The dog follows as we walk away until the woman whistles and calls him over. The dog barks for the first time and runs back home. My heart is heavy after leaving the farm, yet I'm rested, and my strength has returned in part. This does little to calm my trepidation as we distance ourselves further into the woods. If the farmer is correct, and the Germans have entered Longeville at some point the previous day or earlier, enemy units could be anywhere.

More than likely, they have overtaken our progress, and we are essentially surrounded. Sticking to the woods is our best chance at avoiding their attention. That, and a whole lot of luck.

Chapter Twenty
The Chalet

We're a short distance from the farmland when movement in the brush causes us all to halt. Two French soldiers walk through the tree cluster, and when they see our group, the first jumps back. "Jesus," he says, gripping his chest. "I thought you were Germans."

"Are you lost?" Longchamps asks.

They approach. "We're catching up to our unit, heading to Grenoble. Please, can you spare some water?"

"Of course." Longchamps removes his canteen, and I do the same.

"I saw your unit yesterday," I tell them. "You're far behind."

The soldiers take long pulls from the canteen, and one says, "We stayed behind with one of our men, Bonheur. God help him."

"What happened?" Mazas asks.

"He slipped down a steep embankment. Broke his leg and hit his head on a stone. We carried him to a village, but there was little we could do."

"Did he die?"

The second man wipes his mouth with a sleeve and says, "We did all we could. Patched his wounds, but none of us are doctors. We left him in a home, with some food and a full canteen, slipping in and out of consciousness. That was two days ago."

They take another sip and pass back the canteens. "Take more," Longchamps offers. "There's a farmhouse not far from here with a generous host. I'll give you directions; be kind, and I'm sure they will give you a jug of milk and some food."

"We, too, know of a chalet with food and drink for passing soldiers. People from the nearby village bring bread, potatoes, and even meat and coffee. It's a long march." The first man removes his backpack and rifles through it. He pulls out a map and a dark glass bottle. "For your generosity," he says and hands Longchamps the liquor. I peer over his shoulder, reading the light blue and yellow label with the depiction of an eagle flying above pine trees. Pontellier-Anis. Longchamps unscrews the cap and takes a nip. His face contorts, and he passes it to me. The liquor burns my throat, but it's good all the same.

Batist steps forward and hands them four packs of cigarettes. Despite our struggle to find food and water, we still maintain more cigarettes than our group could smoke in months. I'm again reminded of our ignorance when leaving the warehouse. So much food … canned fish, dried meat, loaves of bread, wheels of cheese. To think, we'd assumed that we would be safe in Dijon within two days. What a pitiful notion. I will never again be caught so unprepared … that being if we survive this ordeal.

"I can't thank you enough," one of the men says, taking the cigarette packs. We compare maps, then offer them the best of luck.

"Last chance to join us," Mazas tells them. "Walking to Grenoble is a foolish pursuit."

They dismiss his proposition. "Our unit is expecting us. We don't want them to think the worst has happened."

With that, we wave and go our separate ways.

***

The days have been warm in the sun yet crisp from the mountainous altitude. Despite the rough terrain, there is little complaining other than the occasional, "My feet are fucking killing me," and, "Can we rest soon?" The griping is much less than during the march up the mountain. I keep thinking about that blustery night, the way my mind slipped to the brink of darkness, and my body couldn't, wouldn't move. If not for Mazas, I would have closed my eyes and accepted the frigid embrace of the wilderness floor.

It's hard not to dwell on my failures as the hours tick by. If I died that night on the mountain, or any night for that matter, would my trapeze troupe back in Paris find a third member? Would they continue to perform without me? Am I already replaced despite being promising otherwise? Perhaps they are performing now for Wehrmacht soldiers at Moulin Rouge or Medrano … I wonder if their contraption is complete, the odd blueprint of interconnecting ladders and scaffolding that promised to be the height of daring showmanship … I wonder what my replacement looks like …

"It's not far," Longchamps says, snapping my focus to return. "The chalet the soldiers told us about. We're close."

"They'll never make it to Grenoble." Mazas shakes his head. "Even if they do, what's the point? The Germans will already be there."

We all agree, but there is nothing to be done.

After a short break in a clearing with a marvelous vista of green, rolling hills, we return to the woods. It's not long before Longchamps says, "Up ahead," and points. The building is unmistakable through a veil of pine trees atop an embankment. We approach in silence, mindful of the large white rocks along the bumpy ground, like demonic bones of the earth reaching out from their soil confines.

The building is painted a drab gray. Longchamps is first at the door, and before he opens it, we gather to listen. I lean close and inspect an illustration on the panel of a little farm with the words, *Auberge de La Jeunesse*, written above. Horses snort and nicker somewhere farther down the mountainside, but there is no noise inside the cabin.

"I don't hear anything," I whisper. Mazas nods his agreement, and we all eye the doorknob until Longchamps turns the handle. A draft of warm air greets us, and we filter inside. "Hello?" I say, looking about. The cabin is one large room with an open kitchenette in the back and bunk beds lining either wall. There is a doorway in the rear, which Brissanet inspects, then turns and says it's a bathroom. The cabin's center is consumed by a long table that can seat twice our number, and atop the table is a full round of cheese and two loaves of bread. Dirty hands tear into the food, fingers covered in cuts, broken nails encrusted in grit. Longchamps says, "Hold on, just hold on! There's enough for everyone. Let's sit and eat."

"Look over here," Mazas says from the kitchenette. "There's a basket of eggs." He holds one to display. The brown shell is uneven, with something of a fold in it. "Hate to be the chicken that laid this," he says, and we all laugh, dropping our gear and sitting at the table or finding plates and silverware.

When the door opens, we all turn in silence. A woman enters, holding something significant and covered in a cloth over her shoulder. She's burdened by the weight, which looks as if it could crush her feeble frame. Brissanet stands to help her, but she motions him away. "Sit, sit," she says. Her aged face is lined by years of hard work, and she looks us over with a stern gaze. "There's a lot of you."

"Is this your cabin?" Mazas asks.

She shakes her head. "It's everyone's cabin. I walk up the hill twice daily, sometimes three times, to deliver food. There are always more of you. Sometimes one or two, other times groups, such as yourselves."

"We can't thank you enough," Longchamps says, and we all praise the old woman. She tells us to stop and makes a shooing motion with her free hand to clear us from the kitchen counter, then drops her burden. It makes a smacking sound as it falls on the butcher block. The cloth is pulled aside, revealing a tremendous slab of meat. Ripe, red, and marbled with fat.

"Oh my," I say, the words slipping out unintendedly. Meat. Protein. A life taken to provide for others. Tears well at the edges of my eyes.

The old lady smiles. "I was heading up when I heard clambering at the door. I suspected a large party, so I returned and got a substantial cut." She pats the meat, her bent and bony fingers caressing the top. Then, she finds a knife in a drawer and begins cutting sections into manageable portions with the precision of a butcher. "There are potatoes in the cupboard." She points the knife blade. "Get to peeling."

Brissanet removes a sack of potatoes, and Voulard and I help peel and then slice them into wedges. Oil is heating on the stove, and the potatoes are ready to be fried.

"You two." The lady points her knife at Longchamps and Mazas. "Go outside, down the path, and to the right. There's a vegetable patch; you can't miss it. Pick enough for a salad. Remove the outer leaves only; don't dig up whole plants."

Longchamps and Mazas stand at once and do as the woman commands, thanking her. They leave with a wicker basket.

The woman cooks the steaks in butter, and we fry the potatoes. Longchamps and Mazas return, and Longchamps says, "We could see your village from the garden. It's closer than I thought."

The woman nods, adding a chunk of meat to the butter. It sizzles at once, issuing thick clouds of fragrant, earthy steam that drives me mad with hunger. She adds large sprigs of rosemary, sage, and thyme to the butter, along with whole cloves of garlic and sliced onion, and spoons the sizzling mixture over the top of the meat. The tops crisp with the boiling mixture.

"You have to be careful," she says. "The Wehrmacht are in La Creusot, and I've heard Longeville, and Jougne. If that's true, we are basically in Germany right now."

Longchamps grumbles and says, "Never. Never will France be part of Germany."

The woman shrugs. "They have taken the country. France has fallen."

"Maybe it has. But I will never accept a new government's rule or call Germany my homeland. It will always be France." He makes a spitting motion to his side without actually spitting. The woman gives him a stern look, and he apologizes at once.

"The Swiss border is close," the woman says, changing the tone of the conversation. "They're taking in soldiers while there are still soldiers able to cross the border. Once the Germans arrive at the crossings, it will be too late. You will have to travel fast. If you have a map, I will point out some easier paths through the woods."

"Thank you," Longchamps says, his tone subdued. "Everything you have done, everything you continue to do for us, for France; it is not without sincere gratitude and appreciation."

The meat is cooked and heaped on a dish. The potatoes are fried until light brown and piled in bowls. We sit, and everyone gets a steak, a more significant cut than the top restaurants in Paris serve. At that moment, no chef in the world could prepare the meat any better.

Sitting with my unit, my soldiers, my friends, I realize they are the closest thing to family that I might ever have again. And although the mood is cheerful, we begin the meal in quiet contemplation. Some cry. Ross beside me is one of them. No one offers support. It's fair to be left alone in reflection. My emotions run in circles, nearing euphoria at tasting the savory juices that burst with each chew, coating my tongue and throat in protein-laden delight. But there is melancholy in the meal, a memory of things lost, of meals shared with mothers and fathers, people now gone. Special occasions and everyday suppers, all of which were taken for granted. I would do anything to be back in Charolles, alongside my mother and stepfather at the table.

I would never again protest when asked to help in the field or to feed the chickens, longing instead to be in the city gyms and practicing my acrobatics. Chores and upkeep would be done in delight, primarily since my stepfather's sight slowly decreased with age until he became nearly blind. So much responsibility was put on my mother's shoulders. It is she who tills the fields. It is she who sheers the lambs and harvests the produce. Of course, my stepfather helps as best he can, but there isn't much he can do. He still brings in the wine deliveries and navigates the sheep to their pens by touch. Still, my mother has taken on the arduous task of maintaining our little farm.

My mother, if she is still alive—if the horrible Nazis have not taken our land, our food …. killed my family … she must be sick with worry over me. News of Paris's fall will surely have reached her by now, by neighbor or radio. There is a real and terrible possibility that they have been killed. The Germans might have shot them without the slightest provocation.

And here I am, sipping wine from a glass with a mug of hot coffee beside it. My heart aches to hug my mother tight, smell the lilacs in her hair from the soap she makes, feel the warmth of her embrace. But I cannot, and the fault lies on the shoulders of the German army and the Nazi party. Those monsters! Those terrible fiends! Why are they doing this? Why do they lust for the world, to destroy, kill, maim, cripple, and torture all who stand before them? What devil possesses a man to believe such atrocities are warranted and murder inconsequential? I will never forgive them. In my mind, my family is gone. Killed. Shot. Raped. Tortured.

France is destroyed, utterly defeated, without fighting to its capacity. And now, the Germans are keen on expanding their reach to encompass the world and have the gumption to do so. Without France, the only real force opposing them is England, and what can they do from across the ocean? They will fall, eventually. If America joins, then a strong resistance can be formed. But like the last war, the Americans are keen on waiting on the sidelines for us and England to fight until we are stretched beyond capacity and then come rushing to our aid. If they had joined at the beginning, then perhaps—

The door swings open, and a middle-aged man bursts inside. He slicks his sweat-soaked hair out of his eyes and panics, "Quiet, everyone! Turn off the stoves and burners, and shutter the windows!"

The old woman looks at him, startled. "What is it, Jean?"

We all stand from the table, grinding out our cigarettes and doing as he instructs.

"The Germans are on the road below!" he says in a panic.

Chapter Twenty-one
Monday, 24 June, 1940

A debate bordering on an argument strikes up.

Ross says, "We need to leave, go back to the woods." Those wanting to flee are in small number. Longchamps says, "There are a dozen paths from the village into the woods, and I am willing to guess this is not the only cabin in the vicinity, is it?" He looks to the woman.

"No. There are plenty about if you know where to look." She ties a headkerchief over her hair, tucking in loose gray strands.

"Exactly," he continues. "If you know where to look. We are just as safe, if not safer, inside than outside."

Most of us nod in agreement, but Ross makes a loud counterargument.

"Quiet," I tell him. "We all need to be quiet, whether we stay or not."

Ross looks at me and then shakes his head. "If the consensus is to stay, so be it." He reclines back in a chair and fishes a cigarette from his front pocket. Brissanet sits beside a front-facing window with the shutter cracked open, and Mazas sits beside a window facing the side. The middle-aged man and the woman leave, telling us someone will return when the road is clear.

A wedge of cheese is left, and we cut away pieces with our knives while we wait. The flesh is firm and silky, laden with salt crystals that crunch and explode with flavor. I can't give up the opportunity to eat while there is food, so I cut paper-thin slivers and let them sit on my tongue.

Longchamps and Voulard wash the dishes, and Weber uses a towel to dry them before putting them back in the cabinet. When they are finished, they join us at the table, and we all smoke cigarettes while the cheese dwindles to rind, which is also eaten.

"Someone's coming," Brissanet whispers while waving for our attention. We turn to him, and some grind their cigarettes in ashtrays. Then he lets out a held breath and sits back down. "It's the lady." The room seems to contract in a collective sigh of relief.

Longchamps opens the door for her, and she says, "It's safe. Go now, before they return." She's holding two baskets of eggs. "Take this one with you. They're boiled. The others are for the next group when they arrive, which may be less frequent as the Germans now surround us."

We gather our gear, and Mazas holds out a thick fold of money. "Here," he says. "Please, take it."

The woman offers open palms, refusing. "It's not necessary."

"I insist. If at least to buy more supplies. We have no need for it."

"It would pain me to take it. Go now, boys, and may God be with you."

One by one, we hug the woman, and I feel tears emerge when it's my turn, and also feel her tears against my neck as we embrace. Her thin figure, her frail form; she is all of our mothers, wives, aunts, and grandmothers, and we walk outside speechless. "There goes a good woman," Longchamps says, his eyes red.

***

The vista is stunning. Tall pine trees span in all directions, along with shorter shrub-like trees with yellow leaves. The walk is easy, but I wonder if the recent food makes it feel hospitable, and the near starvation which made every small rock a deadly obstacle. A low stone wall guides our path, with the top fenced in barbed wire and markers placed in distant intervals. I inspect one, a stone pillars about four feet tall, with a vivid crest carved in the side and painted red, blue, and white. Dates are carved into the stone and painted red: *1824* on one side and *1648* underneath the crest.

The stone marker is rough and cool against my fingers, and I nearly collide with Mazas in front of me, who has stopped short. "What—" is all I get out when I look up and see a cabin on the opposite side of the short wall, far down in the low of a valley. Uniformed men stand in front. When I see the sloped helmets and buttoned-up jackets, they look German. But after inspection, their fatigues are unmistakably Swiss.

"Have we …" I say. "Is this it? Have we made it?"

No one moves. We stare at the dozen or so armed soldiers. There are civilians among them wearing Red Cross armbands. A soldier spots us and whispers to a man beside him, and then they both look our way and wave us over. "Hey!" one yells, "Are you French?"

"Yes," Longchamps shouts in reply. "Can we … we would like to enter Switzerland!"

"Walk," the soldier shouts. "Cross the border!"

We walk fast, and some of us run to a turnstile built into the wall so that people can cross, but cattle cannot. Ross and Jerome don't bother but step awkwardly over the barbed wire, the cuff of Ross's pants pinch and rip free. I find myself running once on the other side, across a grass field, to where the Swiss soldiers walk to meet us. "Is anyone injured?" one calls out.

"No," Longchamps says.

The cabin is small and brown, with red window shutters. A sign mounted above a window reads, *Cas Mont d'Or*. The wooden door has a Swiss flag painted on it, with a deer's head above. The inscription reads, *Club Alpin Suisse, 1863*.

"Come with me," a Swiss soldier says, leading us down an embankment. Thick fog filters through the bordering woods from what I believe to be a river below, though I cannot see it. The mist seems to creep into my mind, distorting my thoughts, because I'm in disbelief that we are in Switzerland.

"That's all it took." Mazas shakes his head, and a tear drops. "A stone wall, not tall enough to stop a child. One step over, and we are safe. One step back, and we will be shot …

I don't respond. I cannot. Words won't pass the lump in my throat.

When we reach a trodden path at a level section of the mountain, people come running to meet us. Girls, all French, who have also reached refuge. They want to carry our bags and ask about our journey, where the Germans are, and if we are okay, injured, are we hungry, thirsty, and what our addresses are back home so word can be sent of our safety. Hands inspect bruises and wounds, as well as holes in uniforms. It is all too much, and I cry but try not to. I cover my face as I walk, and soft, loving hands embrace me.

Epilogue

I must have listened to Beethoven's 7th Symphony a thousand times while writing this novel. Even now, writing this epilogue, it is playing in the background. There's something dynamic about that piece of music, the second part in particular, that meshes with this story. I can only hope that a small fraction of that impactful symphony transcended to these pages.

Thank you for reading *Bird Without a Cage*. If you haven't yet guessed, 'Zenner,' as he's called in the book, is my grandfather. Bernard Zenner. This story is his own, and not mine, but only mine to tell through fiction. As mentioned in the story, he kept a diary as his unit endured countless days evading the German Army. Shortly after he arrived in Switzerland, his story was published in a Geneva Newspaper. A Soldier's Story, it was called, or something to that effect. Now, decades later, and well after five years of research and writing, the book is finished. But you know that already because you're still reading.

The best way to support an independent author is by leaving a review. If you enjoyed *Bird Without a Cage*, I would appreciate it if you do so. Be ready for the second part of this story, in book II, *High Wire Act*. Bernard's story has only just begun. Check my Amazon page for all new and old work, and reach me at brandonzenn@gmail.com, if you like. My Instagram is @brandonzen.

Okay. That's it. Goodbye.

Sincerely,

Brandon Zenner